A Candlelight Ecstasy Romance®

"YOU MISS YOUR WEALTHY FRIENDS, YOUR FANCY CARS AND PARTIES, DON'T YOU, ALISON?" JAKE ACCUSED.

"You're just too good to work in a stable and get your hands dirty—"

"That's enough! You're a bigger snob than I am, Jake Koske. You say I can't stand living this way, but what you're really thinking is that I don't have what it takes. I'm not tough like you." Her stare was icy cold. "But I think you're afraid that maybe I *can* make it. That maybe I can turn this filthy place into a home."

"Lady," he sneered, "you won't last a week."

"That's a challenge I can't refuse. I'll show you I can take anything you dish out, no matter how miserable you try to make me. I'm staying, whether you like it or not!"

CANDLELIGHT ECSTASY ROMANCES®

HANDS OFF
THE LADY

Elise Randolph

A CANDLELIGHT ECSTASY ROMANCE®

Published by
Dell Publishing Co., Inc.
1 Dag Hammarskjold Plaza
New York, New York 10017

ISBN: 0-440-13427-7

Printed in the United States of America

March 1986

10 9 8 7 6 5 4 3 2 1

WFH

To Our Readers:

We have been delighted with your enthusiastic response to Candlelight Ecstasy Romances®, and we thank you for the interest you have shown in this exciting series.

In the upcoming months we will continue to present the distinctive sensuous love stories you have come to expect only from Ecstasy. We look forward to bringing you many more books from your favorite authors and also the very finest work from new authors of contemporary romantic fiction.

As always, we are striving to present the unique, absorbing love stories that you enjoy most—books that are more than ordinary romance. Your suggestions and comments are always welcome. Please write to us at the address below.

Sincerely,

The Editors
Candlelight Romances
1 Dag Hammarskjold Plaza
New York, New York 10017

CHAPTER ONE

"I refuse to be poor, and that's all there is to it."
Alison McKinsey, basking in the image of herself,
preened before the mirror in her foyer. Mirror
was really too humble a label for this extravagant
gilt-framed monstrosity of glass that hung in perfect alignment above the credenza. Below it, fresh
flowers floated in an ancient lacquer bowl her father had picked up on one of his many jaunts to
China. A jade frog hunkered on the bottom of the
bowl. Actually, all of the decor in this condomin-
ium was a reflection of both the woman who
owned it and the locale. Alison McKinsey and New
York City—a brash, outrageous, and irresponsible
duo.

The painting of another woman that hung over
the fireplace was reflected in the mirror, and in a
subconscious desire to be like her beautiful and
delicate mother, Alison began to fret with her red
hair.

The man's voice behind her was gentle but
blunt. "All this fussing with yourself won't change
a thing and you know it."

Alison turned around and glared at William

Sipes. He was standing across the room, rattling the keys and change in his pants pockets, a sure sign that he was uneasy as always with the shocking conglomeration of reds in her living room. It was expensively decorated—with that no one could argue. But its bizarre color scheme made most of her guests feel off-balance, as if they were walking on a tilted floor in a carnival funhouse, never knowing which door to enter or which wall was real and which was only an elaborate illusion.

She reached for her cashmere jacket and slipped it on, checking her collar in the mirror. "They say Jeffrey Colfax is broke too, but he never misses a Friday night at The Palm. He was last seen cruising about in that black Ferrari of his."

"You are not Jeffrey Colfax," William said.

Alison spun around angrily. "Then why don't you stop pussyfooting around and tell me exactly what you mean when you say I'm broke?" She picked up a travel brochure that lay on the credenza. "Are you saying this cruise is too expensive?" She added emphatically, "I will not go tourist class."

William Sipes, on the downside of fifty, always looked worried, but that was primarily due to the rapid thinning of his hair, which he constantly patted and stroked in hopes that his attentive caresses would delay the inevitable. Despite his impeccably tailored three-piece suit and his equally impeccable reputation as partner in one of the more prestigious law firms in the city, he was now frustrated to the extreme.

"Trust," he mumbled, shaking his head. "That's

what your father had in me . . . he trusted me with his estate. It's the same thing I've been trying to tell you for I don't know how many years." He paused and shook his head again. "Somehow I have failed."

"Oh, William, stop being so dramatic. You're much too hard on yourself. You're a wiz at law, a trusted friend." She laughed softly. "A bit of a fussbudget, but . . ."

"You can't go with your friends on this trip, Alison."

The smile faded from her face and she stared at him.

"I always go somewhere at the end of May," she said. "Always."

"You don't have the money."

"A simple little vacation, William . . ."

"Your whole life has been one long vacation, Alison." William was pacing, his dark wingtip shoes intersecting the white glare of sunlight that spilled through the window across the dark oak floor. "I've been warning you for years, advising you to watch the spending, all the extravagance and frivolity." He stopped and stared across that disconcerting space of red that separated them. "You haven't listened," he cried in agitation. "You've frivoled it all away."

"Frivoled!" Alison laughed, obviously not taking the man seriously. "Really, William, there's no such word."

"It fits."

She sighed and sat down on the arm of the magenta couch. "All right, so what am I supposed to do about this—this little setback? I've already dropped my maid service to only two days a week and—why are you shaking your head?"

"Because you—or rather I—have dropped your maid service altogether." He began speaking more rapidly now, as if he wanted to get a bad taste out of his mouth. "As well as your monthly trips to the spa, your restoration on this town house—which is as of tomorrow on the market—and your trip to the Azores or wherever it is you had planned to go, and your Maserati, and—"

"My car!" Alison plopped onto the couch and her expression melted against the red backdrop. "You sold my car!"

"Yes."

She stared at him as the truth slowly sank in and her voice was childlike and full of pained awe, as if she had just been told there was no Santa Claus. "Let me get this straight, William. Are you actually telling me that—that I'm poor? That I have no money?"

Like a deflating balloon, William's silent answer settled in a slow sigh upon the room.

"What about my trust? I've only received half of it."

"You remember the terms of the will, Alison. Don't you?"

"Of course," she answered crisply. "I was to get half of the estate at age twenty—which I did, and then the other half is to be handed over when I'm thirty. That's only two years away. Surely—surely I can have an—an advance or something."

William looked down his nose at her. "The second half of the estate was to be yours at thirty—only if you showed some initiative, some McKinsey initiative, in making something on your own. Only if you displayed some of your father's good business sense. Otherwise, that second half of the estate was to go into one of the charitable funds he set up. He was not going to allow you to squander it away."

Her legs were crossed and her foot was now tapping soundlessly in midair. "Initiative."

"That's right. I've been telling you that since you were twenty."

"McKinsey initiative."

"Yes."

"Oh, William," she sighed in exasperation. "You know as well as I do that Daddy was a workaholic. I'm . . . well, I'm just . . ."

"Your father's family came to this country with nothing. Nothing. They were poor Irish immigrants, but he worked his tail off. Constantly, yes. Because of that drive and that ambition, look how far he came. Look at what he was able to give to you."

After a moment she stood up, but immediately lost the energy and sat back down. Prosperity and its material advantages had always defined her life. She didn't know about the hard times. They had all been long before she was born. She had been a part of the season of plenty. Now she was at a loss for she had absolutely no idea how one went about being poor. "Exactly how much . . ." She cleared her throat and tried again. "Exactly how much do I have left?" Her teeth ground together

11

as she waited like a child in the dark for the closet door to burst open and the monster to fly out at her.

William sat down on the edge of a chair across from her. "A little cash in the bank—enough to squeak by for a few months. I'll turn over the latest statement to you."

"And?" she asked, waiting breathlessly, positive there had to be more.

"And this." He handed her a large manila envelope.

She stared at it for a moment, glancing back at him with suspicious gray eyes. She opened it up and pulled out a photograph.

"A horse!" she said, staring at the picture in her hands, then looking up for confirmation that this was what she thought it was and not a symbol for something more abstract, more impressive, more distinguished. But William's face told her that this was it. What she saw was actually a horse. "A horse?" she asked again. "You mean—no stocks? No land? No—no oil wells?" Her fingernails began to drum against the crisp paper. "This is all I have left? Just a stupid horse!"

William glanced at those perfectly manicured red nails tapping incessantly against the manila envelope. He cleared his throat. "I don't know how stupid it is, Alison. It's a Standardbred, a pacer, purchased as a colt a little over a year ago."

"I don't remember buying any racehorse."

"Your brokers handle all of your investments. You didn't want to worry yourself with all of that, remember?"

"No," she asserted, obviously remembering but refusing to let on that she did. "Besides, if they were handling my investments, why am I now sinking into impoverishment?"

William folded his hands together in his lap and pursed his lips in a stern, fatherly fashion. "Think back, dear, to all the times you directed them to sell your stocks so that you could take another trip, to sell your shares in commercial property so that you could refurbish the town house or buy another car. I kept telling you—"

"So how much is this nag worth?" Alison interrupted hotly, not wanting to think back on anything. Alison was not a philosopher. She was a doer. She did not look back. She moved forward.

William checked the file he had brought along with him. "It was purchased as a yearling for fifty thousand."

Alison finally stopped tapping and sat up straight on the couch. "That's wonderful! Then I'll just sell it. I can get by for a few months on fifty thousand, can't I? And when my town house is sold . . ."

"The money will go to pay off your debts," William answered.

"Oh. I see. And the horse?"

"The other owner was contacted and he apparently doesn't want to sell."

Alison frowned at him. "Other owner? What other owner?"

William checked the file again. "Jake Koske is his name. You each own half interest in the horse."

"Koske?" She scowled. "I don't know any Koske. And why doesn't he want to sell?"

"I'm not sure. But there is an interesting footnote here in the file. It took the investment firm three weeks even to locate the guy. Doesn't appear to have a phone—doesn't even seem to have an address. He lives at some fairgrounds—let's see . . ." He flipped to another page in the folder. "Willard County. That's where the horse is stabled."

"Where in blue blazes is that?"

"Illinois."

"Illinois," she repeated dully. To Alison, the entire Midwest represented some vast gray wasteland that one must fly over to reach Vail or Aspen, and her vacuous expression now indicated as much. "Well, someone, I suppose, is just going to have to go there and convince this hayseed to sell." An idea suddenly came to her and she smiled, an irresistible kind of smile, the one men always fell for, the one William always fell for.

This time, he didn't fall. "I can't, Alison," he said, shrugging. "My caseload is full."

Her mouth drew into a thin, petulant line. "Then what about this hotshot investment firm? What am I paying them for?"

William's clearing his throat was a sure sign that he was embarrassed by her question. "You're not. They made it clear that you are—uh—no longer on their list of charitable contributions."

She regarded the attorney for a long moment, absorbing all the new realities in her life. "So," she

14

said, "I have this paltry amount of cash in the bank and this—this animal. That is all, correct?"

William looked sheepish as he pulled an envelope from his pocket. "There is this," he said, handing it over to her.

She opened it and pulled out an airline ticket. "Quincy, Illinois? A rental car?" She looked up at William, studying him for a long moment. "How—how did you know that I would go?"

He shrugged. "Because you have no choice. If you don't go—if you don't prove you can be responsible with money—if you don't try to make something out of what little you have left, then you will end up with nothing. If I were the only trustee of the estate, things might be different. But there are other trustees to satisfy. So, if you don't fulfill the requirements of the trust, you will not receive the second half of your father's estate." He sighed and shrugged again. "Besides, you're Jonathon McKinsey's daughter."

"I'm not my father, William."

He smiled enigmatically. "Not yet, anyway. But, as you said a while ago, you are not about to be poor."

She stood up and adjusted the coat. "So," she mumbled, checking in the mirror to make sure her lipstick was not smudged, "which half of this nag do I own anyway?"

"What was that?"

She sighed. "Oh, never mind." She already knew. With the way her luck was going it had to be the bum half.

CHAPTER TWO

It might as well have been the Australian outback, as much trouble as it was to get there. First it was a commercial plane to Chicago. Tourist class. She was squeezed in beside a woman and her two-year-old daughter who never stopped asking when they were going to get there and who, during mealtime, flipped a spoonful of buttery potatoes onto Alison's aquamarine gabardine skirt.

After that delightful leg of the trip, there was a three-hour wait in O'Hare, then a twin-engine flight to Quincy. The seats were granite hard and packed so closely together that she was reminded of the twenty-four-hour est session she had been forced to endure last year with her friend Megan.

In the Quincy airport she rented a subcompact economy car (one that William would no doubt label sensible), and asked directions to Bartholomew, the seat of Willard County.

Lying before her was an empty stretch of two-lane highway, with little change in the scenery except for a mottled bluff here and a thin, brown creek there. It was all farmland, all a series of green-and-yellow patchwork. Fields lay green with alfalfa and new sprouts of beans. Big orange flowers on tall green stalks bordered the highway. In the distance, farmhouses squatted like roosting hens in the shelter of poplars lined up as windbreaks, their storage bins and barns lopsided and in sad need of a coat of paint, their yards littered with water and propane tanks, old rusted Mustangs or pickup trucks, and sheets hung on the lines to dry.

Alison clutched the steering wheel, holding fast to something tangible in this alien world. She turned on the radio, but switched it back off when she could find nothing but the wail of sad country songs and the morning hog report.

"Why are you here, Alison! Why!" She slapped the steering wheel with her hand and tried once again to make sense of what was happening in her life. She was wealthy. She always had been. It was absurd to think that she was going to have to scrounge around for money.

That was exactly what it looked as if she was going to have to do. She hoped that if she could get her partner to agree on selling the horse, she could take her half of the money and invest it somewhere. First of all, she had to talk the hick into selling, and she had to find him before she could talk him into anything.

She reached the edge of Bartholomew and slowed her car to a sedate twenty-five miles per hour as she entered the small town. A cemetery with crooked headstones was on the left, a farm-implement dealership on the right. There were white framed houses with big front porches, their

17

front lawns dotted with ceramic yard ornaments and burgeoning flower beds. She passed a general store that advertised everything from sacks of feed to the U.S. Mail. A Civil War–vintage cannon made its last stand on the courthouse lawn.

Alison pulled into a Shell station and had the car filled with gas. A teenage boy stood beside the car window snapping his gum, waiting for the money.

"How might I find the fairgrounds?" she inquired politely.

The attendant scratched his head and fixed her with a look reserved for anyone who had just landed from Mars.

"The fairgrounds?" she asked again.

"You see that stop sign there? You go through that one—then at the next you turn that way toward the Baptist church."

"Turn right," Alison repeated.

"Yup. You go to the Baptist church—then hang a right and keep on goin'. You can't miss it—I guarantee it."

"I'm sure you do," she mumbled under her breath as she paid him for the gas. William had cut up all of her credit cards into useless little pieces and now she was burdened with a wad of bills. She was trying to keep very careful track of everything she spent and it was terrifying to see how fast her "cash in the bank" was dwindling away.

She pulled out of the station and glanced into her rearview mirror. The attendant was still standing there, arms crossed, staring in her wake.

Following his directions, she turned "that way" at the stop sign, found the Baptist church, then "hung a right" and followed the road on out. The fairgrounds were straight ahead, but she stopped just short of them. So much depended on this. Her whole life was at stake here. Her future hinged on this one man's agreement either to buy her half of the horse or to sell out completely with her.

Her heart was pounding, her palms sweaty. "Stop it, Alison. You're being ridiculous," she told herself. Most likely he'll be thrilled that you want to sell. Steeling herself against any doubts, she drove through the fairground's gate and pulled up in front of the Racing Secretary's office, a small metal shed that held no aura of profitability.

She parked the car and walked into the shed. A large woman wearing a housecoat sat behind a cluttered desk. In her hand was a long stick with a hook on it, and as soon as Alison entered the office the woman shoved the end of the stick against the door, closing it. She set it down on the floor, picked up a flyswatter and smacked a winged creature on her desk, set the flyswatter down, and picked up a can of cola. Popping the top on the can, she scrutinized Alison from her chair.

"Help you?"

"I'm looking for a man by the name of Jake Koske. He has a horse stabled here."

"Are you her?"

"Her?"

"His wife?"

Alison shook her head. "No."

"He owe you money?"

"In a sense."

The large woman took several gulps of her drink

19

before answering. "Don't count on getting paid. Number seven. Down at the far end. His tack room is the last door on the right."

"Number seven." Alison nodded, thanked the woman for her time, opened the door, and heard it pushed closed behind her with the stick.

As she drove toward the stable at the end, she noticed several men out on the track, perched on some sort of big carts that were being dragged around by the horses. If this was harness racing, it appeared to her to be a rather tame sport and without much challenge. As long as her horse brought what it was due on the marketplace, she didn't really care about the sport.

She stepped from bright sunlight into the dark stable and made her way cautiously down the long dirt corridor. Stalls lined each side and several horses hung their heads over the gates, slurping at their water buckets. One raised its head as she passed and stared at her with slow, pondering eyes while water dripped from the sides of its mouth. Alison grimaced and looked away.

A stableboy dipped his pitchfork into the wet straw of an open stall and tossed the muck back onto a wheelbarrow, narrowly missing Alison.

She stopped when she reached a closed door at the end of the stable. Last door on the right; it had to be Jake Koske's tack room. Directly across from the door, a young boy stood on the stall gate and leaned over to talk to the horse behind it. But when he turned around, Alison saw that he was not a he, but a little girl. Probably no more than eight, she was dressed in faded dungarees and a

20

short-sleeved plaid shirt. Her shaggy hair was cropped above her ears.

"Hello," Alison said politely with a cautious smile. She never knew what to say to kids.

"Hey yourself," the little girl said as she jumped down from the gate and sauntered over to Alison. "My name's Abe. What's yours?"

"Alison," she said with a confused look. "Your name is Abe?"

"Abeline, really," she said, shrugging. "But I like Abe better—shorter, ya know. Easier. Like you. You should be Ali. See what I mean? Shorter. Easier."

"Yes," Alison murmured as she turned toward the closed door. She knocked, but a low muttered curse greeted her from the other side. Her hand jerked back.

"What do you want?" Abe asked.

"I'm looking for someone. Mr. Koske. He lives here."

"Yeah, I know," she said, hooking her thumbs in the suspenders of her overalls and rocking back on her heels. "But he ain't taking any callers right now."

Alison ignored her and turned to knock again.

"I wouldn't do that if I were you."

She stared down at the little girl. "Oh? And why is that?"

" 'Cause he's entertaining Juanita right now."

What thin smile there had been faded from Alison's face. "Entertaining?" she croaked, gawking at the little girl's rocklike expression.

Abe glanced at the man's watch she was wearing. "Let's see, he started on her about . . ." She counted around the dial with her finger. "Forty-five minutes ago."

"St-started on her! How can—I hardly think that's any way for you to . . ."

"More than likely, he's through now. We can check."

"N-no!" Alison stammered. "Wait! I can come back . . ." But Abe had already reached for the handle and opened the tack room door.

It took a few seconds for Alison's eyes to adjust to the dim light, but when they did her gaze swept across the room. Somehow squeezed into the small space were two cots, a worn stuffed chair, a counter with sink, a refrigerator, and shelves above. On the floor was a rag rug, littered with a half-dozen empty liquor bottles and other garbage. Against the far wall a man was propped up on the rust-stained mattress of a rollaway bed. In his right hand was a tall glass and dangling from his left was an empty bottle of tequila.

Alison saw all life as she had known it pass before her eyes and fade away.

Jake Koske stared back at the woman occupying his doorway, seeing her remotely, hazily, as if he were in a dark tunnel and she were standing in the circle of light at the end. She had red hair and was dressed like a stranger. That much he could tell. No one around here wore high-heeled shoes. He didn't want any company right now. Abe knew that. He turned to the girl and growled, "What the hell's going on, Abe? Thought I told you I was busy with Conchita."

Unruffled by the voice, Abe sat down in the stuffed chair. "You said Juanita."

"Yeah?" He lifted the bottle of tequila to his eyes and studied it. "Yeah, Juanita." He looked back at Abe. "So what are you doing in here?"

She thumbed toward Alison. "This broad wanted to see you."

Alison's mouth dropped open and she spun toward the girl. "Br-broad! I don't believe you, you little . . ."

Abe shrugged and stood up, walked over to the man's bed and sat down beside him. She rested her small hand on his denim-covered thigh.

Alison's gaze swung from the rustic drunk to the scruffy little girl beside him. "She belongs to you?"

Jake dropped the tequila bottle to the floor and stretched his long legs out and over the side of the bed. His feet hit the floor with a thud and he leaned forward to cradle his head. "She's mine," he groaned.

"Are you Jake Koske?"

He kept his head cupped between his hands, staring at the floor. "Who wants to know?"

"My name is Alison McKinsey." She waited for a response from him, but none came. "We own a horse together," she added.

He lifted his eyes slowly toward that bright rectangular light where she stood. "That right?" He leaned back against the wall and his foot tapped the tequila bottle, sending it rocking back and forth across a floor plank between them. "What'd ya say your name was?"

"McKinsey. Alison McKinsey."

"So what do you want?"

"I came here to talk over some business with you."

Jake moaned and leaned forward, cradling his head once again. "My office is closed. Get me some aspirin, Abe."

The little girl immediately stood up and moved to the sink. She stood on tiptoes and reached for the medicine on the shelf, opened the bottle, and poured a couple of pills into her hand.

"Why do you call her Abe?" Alison asked, watching Jake toss the pills into his mouth and down them with a glass of water.

"That's her name," he said. "What the hell else would I call her?"

Alison let out a sigh of disgust and looked about the room. Above the smaller cot was a photograph of Jake and Abe, both dressed neatly and smiling happily. There was space on the other side of Abe for another person, but that had been unevenly and haphazardly cut off the picture. She looked back at the man and his daughter. "I'm here because I want to sell the horse, Mr. Koske."

"That so?"

"I thought if we could arrive at a fair price, we could offer it for sale."

Abe shot off the bed like a bullet, her face stiff with righteous indignation. "Bitty ain't for sale. Tell her Jake—tell her."

Jake ran his hand gently up Abe's arm to her shoulder, patting her lightly. "Any beer in there, kid?"

Abe glared at Alison for one hostile second and

24

then stomped to the refrigerator, yanked it open, and pulled out a Pabst Blue Ribbon. She popped the top and tossed it toward the trash can, but it missed its mark. No one seemed to mind; certainly no one bothered to pick it up. She handed the beer to Jake.

He was just tipping it back to take the first swig when that shadowy figure moved out of the light, wrenched it from his hands, and slammed it to the counter.

"Mr. Koske," Alison snapped. "As hard as it obviously is for you to maintain sobriety, I want to get this settled. I've flown halfway across the country and driven a hundred of the most uninspiring miles I've ever seen to get here. Now, please—can't we settle on a price and offer the horse for sale?"

He was staring at Alison as if she were the most peculiar creature he had ever laid eyes on. Then he frowned at the beer she had taken from him. "Maintain sobriety," he repeated dully. "This is one for the book," he mumbled to Abe, keeping his eyes on Alison. "No need to use big words around here, Miss McKinsey. We're country folk. You can talk straight to us."

"Okay," she said between clenched teeth. "See if this is plain enough. I want to sell the horse."

"You heard Abe," he said. "Bittersweet isn't for sale."

"Whose decision is that?"

"Her owner's. Mine."

Alison's fists had moved to her waist. "I am half

owner, Mr. Koske. I have an equal say in the matter."

He was shaking his head. "Nope."

"Nope what?"

He looked straight at her with sober brown eyes, not a trace of intoxication now visible. "Nope, you're not half owner. And nope, you don't have equal say."

She began to stammer. "What do you . . . how can you . . . ?"

He rested his head and shoulders against the wall. "You are what is known in the trade as a deadbeat, Miss McKinsey. One who doesn't pay her bills."

She stared at the man on the bed. "What bills?"

"Training fees, for one thing. My training fees. Then there's vet bills, stall rent, feed, taxes and insurance, shoeing. Anything else, Abe?"

"Couple of rub towels and a sponge," she added, still wearing a glum expression.

"Rub towels?" Alison repeated. "Stall rent? This is preposterous!"

"Since I paid for all these things myself," Jake mused, "my side of the ownership tally sheet is considerably higher than yours."

Alison rested her hand against the back of the stuffed chair, but yanked it back when a puff of dust flew from the upholstery. She grimaced at her hand, holding it out from her skirt at an awkward angle. "I had no idea about these charges or I certainly would have paid them."

Jake shrugged and folded his arms across his chest. "All I know is that I kept sending the bills to some address I was given in New York and the bills were never paid. That tells me one of two things, Miss McKinsey. Either my partner doesn't have enough cookies in the cookie jar to cover it, or she's a crook. Either way, I figure I'm in trouble—know what I mean?"

Alison was outraged. "I am not a crook! And I certainly have enough cookies to cover these petty little charges of yours. Now, how much do I owe you? I'll pay you now and then we'll be equal again, right?"

Jake rolled his head from side to side and massaged his stiff neck. He eyed the beer on the counter and wished he wasn't sobering up so fast. He stood up and rested his hand against the wall until the dizziness passed.

Alison watched him stagger over to the counter for the beer. He got it, staggered back to the cot, and sat down.

"Well, let's see," he said, after taking a long, satisfying drink. "There is my training charge of five hundred a month for . . . let's see, you're three months behind on that. Then there's fifty dollars a month for feed, ten dollars for stall rent, two hundred a month for public liability insurance, fifteen dollars for new shoes, a vet bill of . . . let's see, I think that was twenty dollars and . . . how much were those rub towels and sponges, Abe?"

"Four bucks," she said.

"Okay, so that's—you got a calculator, Miss McKinsey?"

Not caring at this point about the filthy chair,

Alison sank into it and let the cloud of dust settle around her. She was silent as she stared at the littered floor of the tack room. Finally she looked up at him. "If . . . when we sell it . . . then I—I could pay you the money you're due."

"She's not for sale," Abe sputtered, glaring at Alison.

Jake leaned forward and held the beer can between his knees. He shook his head. "She's been through enough."

"Who has?" Alison snapped impatiently. She saw Jake glance quickly at Abe, his face tight and unreadable. After a moment, he looked back at her.

"Bittersweet," he said softly. "Besides, she's out of training. Nobody would pay what she's worth unless she's ready to race."

"What would it take to get her ready?"

Jake yawned and massaged his neck again. "You've got to find yourself a trainer."

"You said you were a trainer! You said I owed you training fees."

He shrugged. "You didn't pay . . . so I didn't train."

She sighed, then took a deep breath to calm herself. "Look," she said, slowly and distinctly. "If you will train it, then we can sell it. After we sell, I'll pay you what you are due."

"Only one problem with that, Miss McKinsey." Jake took a long swig on his beer and leaned back on his elbows. "I don't want to do it."

Alison stared at the man across from her. His hair was the color of everything else around this place—brown. The same as his eyes, the same as the shirt he was wearing, the same as the dirt on the floor, and the horses in the stalls, and the track outside. Hadn't anyone here heard of color? Where were the claret reds and the sapphire blues and the cadmium yellows of her world? Was this monotonous brown world all these people knew?

Her gaze swung to the little girl beside Jake Koske. She was sitting ramrod straight on the cot, her small fist clutching her father's shirttail.

She looked at their sullen faces peering out from the closed brown framework of their lives, and she took a deep breath. It definitely looked as if she had her work cut out for her. She was not about to lose out on that inheritance. Come hell or high water, she was going to bring back all the colors and riches to her life. If these two country bumpkins thought she would admit defeat and slink away with her tail between her legs, they were dead wrong. Despite the fact that she had never had to work for anything in her life, she had been bred from a fighter. It was in her genes. And above and beyond that, Alison McKinsey always got her way. Always.

CHAPTER THREE

The sign read EDDIE'S BAR AND GRILL, but the GR
hung down by a wire, leaving the ILL alone and
prophetic. Alison stepped through the doorway
and into the orange haze of the bar. The place
smelled of cigars and grease, and a cloud of thick
gray smoke hung above the griddle where burgers
and dogs were frying. She felt herself jostled aside
as a group of men came through the door behind
her, and the *ping-ping* from the copper spittoons
by the door made it clear someone in the group
had at least hit his mark. A twang of guitar and a
shrill female voice sobbed from the jukebox in the
corner, and a booted foot stomped to the beat at a
nearby table.

Alison stood just inside the door, still wearing
her aquamarine gabardine twill jacket and skirt
with the pale silk blouse, searching across the sea
of cowboy hats, Levi's jeans, and madras shirts for
some familiar guidepost in this uncharted terrain.
She wondered if perhaps, just perhaps, she should
have worn something a teensy bit more casual.

She ignored the openmouthed stares and
walked over to the bar. A couple of men in tractor

30

hats were discussing the latest John Deere Hitch and Harrow.

"Shoot fire, boy," one of them was saying, "all you gotta do is link that crumble roller up to yer universal drive joint and take off. I had those bean rows of mine done in—" He broke off and turned toward the woman sitting on a barstool next to him. "Well, hey there, pretty lady. Buy you a drink?"

Her smile was guarded. "Thank you, no. I—I'm looking for a horse trainer. I understand lots of them hang out here."

The other man pulled his hat off and leaned forward, staring around his friend at her. "This is the place. But what do you want with one of them rowdies?"

She glanced around the bar. "Is there anyone here I could talk to . . . any trainer here tonight?"

The first man cocked his head toward the table at the back. The waitress was setting down a pitcher of beer and picking up the empty. Five men took turns pouring their mugs full. "That table?" she asked.

"Yeah, they're all trainers. And not a one of 'em worth his salt in pay, neither. You'd do well to watch yourself with them."

"Thanks," she said, sliding off the stool. "I'll remember that."

"You gonna be in town . . . ?"

The voice was drowned out by the wail of a mournful song as she walked past the jukebox. She stopped at the table and five pairs of eyes turned

31

toward her. She realized now it didn't matter that she was dressed as if she were going to a luncheon at Tavern-on-the-Green. They were all looking at her as if she were stark naked.

She took a deep breath and clutched her handbag tighter. "I'm looking for a horse trainer," she said.

"What for?" one of them asked.

"Well . . . for my horse."

She laughed nervously along with the men, even though she was pretty sure the laughter was directed at her.

"No kidding," another man said. "Who's your horse?"

"Ah—its—its name is . . ." She had forgotten. But she hadn't imagined that anyone would ask that or even care what the name was. "I forgot," she murmured, amid a new round of laughter. "But it's being kept over at the fairgrounds."

"I don't remember any new horse being brought in," the man closest to her said.

"Well, actually it's been there for a while," she said. "It's . . . well, my partner has been looking after it . . . sort of."

"Who's your partner?"

"Jake Koske," she mumbled, hoping they wouldn't hear her.

"Koske! Him and you own that filly together?"

"Unfortunately, yes, but Mr. Koske has no desire to train the horse right now. So, I'm willing to offer one of you a salary plus a percentage of profits from any races it wins and from its eventual sale."

The man at her end of the table reached out to

touch her, but decided against it at the last second. He let his palm fall to the table in front of her. "Lady, listen, I don't think you quite understand. It's like we said—it's Koske's horse."

"I'm half owner," she asserted.

"Yeah, but he's the trainer."

"But he doesn't want to train it."

"Can't say that I blame him," one of the others said. "I heard the filly ain't got any legs. Waste of time trainin' her."

"Legs!" she huffed indignantly. "Of course it has legs. What kind of an animal—"

"She won't do well in the races," the man nearest her explained.

Another man set his mug of beer down and spoke up. "If Koske thought she'd do good, he'd train her himself. I'm not interested."

"Neither am I," another said. "I've got enough work right now."

"Koske ain't got any money to pay no trainer. You loaded or somethin'?"

"I can pay," she said, her eyes steady and cool with the lie. "That is, if any of you are interested. I want that horse to race this summer and I'm willing to pay for that."

Several pairs of boots dropped to the floor with an echoing thud as they stared at her. "This summer!"

"You want that horse to race this summer?"

"Of course," she insisted.

"Do you have any idea how long it takes to get a horse ready to race?"

A flicker of doubt edged into her expression. "No."

"This is the end of May," the man next to her said. "The races start on the Fourth of July. There ain't no way, lady. No way 'tall."

"Then you're saying that you wouldn't be inter—" She cleared her throat. There was no point in even asking a second time. Their dumbstruck expressions said it all.

With a flourish, Alison signed the register and prayed silently that the manager of the Island in the Sun Motel wouldn't make her pay with cash up front. A plaque on the counter boasted, TELEVISION AVAILABLE. ALL ROOMS CARPETED AND CLEAN.

The woman behind the desk was obviously not impressed with Alison's signature or her aquamarine gabardine twill. "Listen, doll," she said, leaning a round, dimpled elbow on the counter. "No shenanigans are gonna be tolerated here. This is a high-class tourist court. Understand?"

In only a few days she would have been on a cruise ship, swaying across the ocean with a piña colada in her hand, the sun warm on her face, the prospect of a wealthy, attractive man for the evening. . . . She took the key from the woman and carried her bag back out and down the dirt drive to her room. Number seven. The same number as the tack room. And not much cleaner, despite what the sign said.

This had to be the bottom of the barrel. She could not sink any lower than this, she was sure.

While she unpacked, she reevaluated her situation. There really were only two solutions she could think of. Either Jake Koske would agree to sell the horse now—which she doubted at this point that he would do. He and that smart-mouthed brat of his had been so adamant about that. That left only one possible solution. Jake would simply have to train the horse and get it ready to race this summer.

Maybe she had come on a little too strong this afternoon. With the right touch, she was sure she could convince him to do it. After all, he was a man. There had never been a man she couldn't wrap around her little finger. Tonight she would go back to the fairgrounds. Drunken sot or not, he was still a man, and she should have no problem reeling him in.

She stood in the doorway of the tack room and stared hungrily at the pizza Jake and Abe were sharing on the bed. She had forgotten about dinner and now her stomach was reminding her of how long it had been since she had eaten.

Jake took a bite of pizza and glanced up. "She's back. Something we can help you with, Miss McKinsey?"

"I want you to train the horse."

"You came all the way back to say that?" He took another big bite of cheese and pepperoni. "I thought you said that earlier." He looked at Abe. "Didn't she say that earlier?"

"Yep."

He looked back at Alison. "Abe and I remember you saying that earlier."

"Mr. Koske," she said, clenching her teeth to regain her composure. She had this all planned out. She didn't want to spoil it now by getting angry. She let out a slow breath and smiled, the famous Alison McKinsey smile that lit up rooms the minute she walked into them. "Jake . . . listen, I've been thinking. I'm really sorry about this mix-up with the bills. My accountants . . . well, I'm sure I don't have to tell you how they can mess things up. I called them from the motel and let them know exactly what I thought of their services. They will no longer be in my employ, I can assure you that. And, of course, I would be more than willing to pay you your usual training fee, plus—"

"I want all back pay due plus two months in advance."

Alison was stunned. "What!"

"Two months . . . in advance."

She froze in the doorway, a tightly packed bundle of icy molecules. She couldn't pay him what he wanted. She knew that. Her "cash in the bank" wouldn't extend nearly far enough for that. But she couldn't let him know that.

Jake chuckled and looked at his daughter. "I knew it. Didn't I tell you, Abe?"

"You told me."

He chuckled again and shifted his eyes to Alison. "Save your breath, Miss McKinsey. You don't have it."

"That's preposterous!"

He shook his head. "It's written all over you, lady. You've got that desperate look. Help, I'm drowning! That's what your eyes tell me. And you'll grab at any straw in the pond."

"That's insane. That's . . ."

He waved away her outrage. "Look, I'm not in the market for another desperate woman. Okay?"

Alison stared at him, despising him for not succumbing to her charm the way all the men before him had. Where had she gone wrong with this one? Was he too much of a hick to understand how the game was played?

Her eyes flicked over the room. It was still a mess. Abe's cot was unmade and a pair of dirty overalls lay on the floor beside it. Her eyes lifted to the shelf above where the picture was propped against a book. A man and a little girl and a jagged edge where someone else had once been. She looked back at them, sitting on the floor eating their pizza as if she wasn't there. She started to turn, but something made her stop and glance back up at the shelf. The book that held up the picture was turned so the spine faced out. The title was in silver lettering: *Care & Training of the Trotter & Pacer.* She looked back at Jake and Abe. They were ignoring her. They wouldn't even notice if . . .

Slowly extending her arm, she reached for the book, slipping it carefully from behind the picture. The photograph fell facedown as she pulled the book to her and dropped it in her purse.

She turned without a word to either of them and

stepped out of the tack room, walking down the long dark corridor to the end of the stable.

"Did you see that?" Abe asked, with a mouthful of pizza. "Did you see what she took?"

"Yeah." He nodded. "I saw. You gonna eat that last slice, or can I have it?"

The shrill ring of the telephone beside her bed jarred her from a deep sleep, and she groaned and flung her hand toward the irritating noise. She lifted the receiver and her eyes shot open wide at the "Cock-a-doodle-do" that greeted her. There was a heavy scratch, as if a needle had just been wrenched from the record, followed by a woman's voice. "This is your wake-up call. It's six o'clock in the mornin'."

Alison dropped the phone back in place and stared at a patch of peeling paint on the ceiling. The lamp was still on by the bed and when she dropped her gaze to her clothes, she realized she was still dressed. The book lay open on top of her stomach.

Dragging herself up, she padded in stockinged feet across the floor and flicked back the blue-flowered curtain. Across the road was a field, a flat plane of short wheat extending as far as the eye could see. A band of pale pink stretched across the horizon, and above that a morning star faded under the rising light.

"Why am I here?" Alison asked the new dawn. "What am I going to do?"

She looked back at the book lying facedown on the bed. She had read it all. Well, most of it any-

38

way. It was written in a fairly straightforward style, each chapter giving the advice of various horse trainers. "I can do it," she told herself. "After all, if that boozehound Jake Koske can do it, I certainly can. It will just take a little work, that's all." Work. She tried the word several times, letting it roll across her tongue to see how it felt. It was one she had not used very often, a word from another language that described something foreign and bewildering to her. She wasn't at all sure if she liked the sound of it or not. Still . . .

There was no other choice. Koske had no intention of training it, and no one else seemed inclined to jump in either. So that left only her. That old nag was going to race this summer and it was going to make some money—enough at least to make it salable. Once it was sold, Alison could go back to New York and show William and the other trustees how resourceful she had been. McKinsey initiative, and all that. The second half of the estate would be hers, and life as she knew it would be restored once again.

She let the curtain drop back into place and walked over to the bed, picking up the book. This was going to do it for her. This was her salvation. With this she would bring back all the colors in her life.

She felt the slow, dull stares of the horses on her as she made her way down the stable, as if they were already judging her ability to deal with their breed. A snort, sounding much like a human snicker, came from behind one of the stall gates, but when she glanced over she saw only a black horse with a white stripe up its head looking back at her.

The barn was thick with the smell of hay and horse and dry, splintery wood, and Alison swatted several flies away when they tried to land on her. She reached the end stall and stood in front of the gate, staring in at the chestnut horse. Bittersweet, they had called it. It was standing backward with its tail toward Alison and its head hanging in the far corner. With the training book tucked under her arm, Alison made a few little awkward kissing sounds.

The horse didn't even look around.

Alison tried again, snapping her fingers and clicking her teeth and kissing the dry air. "You'd better pay attention, horse." Still staring at nothing but the horse's rear end, she tried another tactic. "Listen, I'm your new trainer, so you had better look at me and listen up."

When there was no reaction, she sighed and stepped closer to the stall, unwrapped the wire that was looped from the rail brace to a rusty nail on the slat fence, and pulled the gate open. She tiptoed up behind the horse.

"She kicks."

Alison spun around to face the small voice.

Abe was standing in the doorway of the tack room, dressed in the same worn dungarees she had been wearing the day before. She hooked her thumbs in the straps of her overalls and rocked back on her heels. "You'd better watch yourself."

Alison's eyes flicked back to the horse's rump. It

was close enough to touch. But she laughed lightly. "No need to try and scare me off. It won't work." She took another step, but froze when a loud puff of air escaped from its nose and a large hoof pawed the hay on the floor. "Kicks?" she asked warily.

Abe shrugged behind her. "Wouldn't want to try and scare you off, though."

Alison slowly backed her way out of the stall and slammed the gate shut just as the horse swung toward her. She quickly looped the wire over the nail and jumped back, heaving a sigh of relief.

"Might help if you'd feed her," Abe muttered, not even trying to hide the disgust in her voice. She stepped down from the room and walked to the wall where three round bins were mounted. She lifted the lid of one and measured out the proper amount of feed into a bucket, carried it to the stall, and dumped it through a hole in the wire mesh where another, larger bucket was hanging. At the sound of the granules hitting the metal bucket, Bittersweet swung toward the pan and began eating. Abe stuck her hand through the mesh and rubbed the horse's forehead.

Alison, still clutching the book in her hands, watched Abe. "I was just about to get around to that, you know."

"Sure." Abe grabbed the water bucket that hung in front of the stall and filled it up at the tap, replacing it on the hook.

The idea of such adultlike cynicism coming from such a tiny body was almost more than Alison could take. But she couldn't think of anything in-

41

telligent enough to counter it. So she shifted from one expensive leather shoe to the other and said nothing. The flies were starting to swarm again and she didn't really think she was going to be able to stand hanging around this filthy stable all day. Still, she didn't have much choice. This was her only solution.

She unbuttoned the cuffs of her yellow blouse and rolled up the sleeves. She caught Abe staring at her, her impenetrable child's eyes taking in the designer belt, the rust linen pants, the soft woven leather of the rust flats she was wearing. Alison felt curiously vulnerable, waiting for something, some comment, some childish question, anything but that knowing stare.

Without comment, Abe moved over to the open doorway, sat down, and began using a stick to remove some horse manure from the bottom of her shoe.

"How long does it take to eat?" Alison asked.

Abe didn't look up from her task. "First of all—it ain't an it. It's a she."

Alison sighed. "Okay. How long does it take for her to eat?"

"That all depends."

Alison listened carefully, knowing she would have to remember every bit of advice she could get if she was going to learn to train this horse properly. "On what?" she asked eagerly, wishing she had a pen and paper.

Abe looked up and tossed the stick to the ground. "On when she gets full."

CHAPTER FOUR

"What in tarnation is all this racket?" The towering figure shaded the doorway, his feet on each side of Abe's hips, his hands braced against the door frame. His hair was mussed, his voice groggy. "What's going on here? Oh, it's you." He leaned sideways against the wooden jamb and rubbed his chest with his hand.

Alison was staring at him as if he had nothing on. Even though he was wearing jeans, the way he stood there bare-chested, gazing at her out of half-opened eyes, made her feel decidedly uneasy. She hadn't realized he was such a big man, so tall and broad-shouldered, and she scowled at the very idea of a man so intimidatingly large. The whole scene was too informal, too intimate, for her taste, so she turned away. But the image of the man with brown eyes and hair and a broad tanned chest lingered in her mind.

She laid her book on a big wooden trunk and opened it to one of the pages she had marked. First, she had to get the horse out of the stall, then she had to hook her to something called crossties. Against the side of the stall a long leash hung down. She looked toward the other wall, her eyes skimming past Jake, and saw the other leash. Those had to be the crossties. Now all she had to do was get the horse out of there.

Ignoring the attentive silence behind her, Alison slowly swung open the gate. She knew they wouldn't offer to help, and that was just fine with her. She had read all about how to do this and she certainly didn't need them.

Bittersweet was wearing a halter, which would make it a little easier to grab hold of her. The training book suggested leaving the halter on at all times, so at least Jake had been sober enough to do that. The book also suggested putting the bridle on in the stall Oh, but how could she stand to walk through the hay and muck to do that!

She reached for the bridle on its hook, gritted her teeth, and stepped into the stall, sinking ankle-deep in the scratchy hay. Bittersweet kept her head toward the feed bucket, but her eyes were trained on every move the woman made. Alison swallowed and took another step, but the horse lifted a front hoof and stamped it into the hay. Alison glanced back at the doorway. Abe was no longer there, but Jake was, and on his face was an amused grin.

I'll show him, she told herself. I'll show that smug hayseed that I can do this as well as he can. How dare he stand there and grin at me! She turned back to Bittersweet and began making small clicking noises with her tongue and murmuring soft entreaties the way she had seen people do in the movies. She reached out tentatively

44

and lightly touched the horse's flank, running her fingers along the surprisingly smooth buttock and thigh. She was a city girl who had never been around horses, and she had no idea what one even felt like.

The horse responded this time and angled around perpendicular to her. Alison continued to stroke her side, lifting up over the withers and sliding down her back across the harness. She touched the harness, but the horse sensed something wrong and stepped back. Alison stepped forward and tried again, running her fingers lightly along the leather strap to accustom the horse to the feeling. Her ankles itched from the dry hay, a thin layer of sweat lay along her neck beneath her hair, and her pulse fluttered erratically in her throat.

"Come on, girl," she said, feeling idiotic but realizing it was probably essential if she wanted to get any closer to the horse. She continued crooning and reached for the harness, this time hooking her fingers beneath it. Bittersweet tried to skirt the touch, but Alison kept a firm grip, all the while stroking and murmuring soft words of encouragement.

The perspiration was gathering at her temples now as she lifted the bridle from where it draped over the gate and held it up to the horse. She had read several times last night how to do this, but suddenly her mind was blank. She couldn't remember anything. She lifted her arm and wiped it across her wet forehead, a gesture that was so unladylike that she would have been shocked if she had realized what she was doing. She concentrated hard, trying to remember what the book said. It was outside the stall—if she could just get it without letting go of the harness. Finally the words on the page formed in her mind. The bit. That went into the horse's mouth first. But the ears, there was something about the ears. Oh, yes, some horses were real fussy about their ears when you pulled the bridle over the head.

Grateful that she had remembered in time, she unbuckled one side of the bit and let it hang down. Then very, very slowly and carefully, she lifted the bridle toward the head, aware of that huge dark eye staring sideways at her. She lifted it higher and then at the last minute let go of the harness and used both hands to slip the bridle onto the head. The horse whinnied and tried to jump back, but Alison kept with her, falling against her side and struggling with the bridle to get it in place.

Alison jumped back, breathing fast and hard as Bittersweet started to circle and stomp. She edged out of the stall and slammed the gate.

Turning around, she saw Jake sitting in the doorway with a beer in his hand and that amused grin still on his face. Abe was seated on the lower step between his legs, combing the hair of a doll. The incongruous mix of tomboy and little girl struck Alison, but she was too busy trying to catch her breath and fuming at the father to pay closer attention to Abe.

"You two are really enjoying this, aren't you?" she snapped.

Abe looked up, but her expression was blank, whereas her father's was positively mirthful.

"You're getting a big kick out of watching me struggle with this—this—beast, aren't you?"

Jake stood up and took two big strides over to the stall. He opened the gate, reached for the bridle, and pulled the horse out into the corridor. Alison pressed herself back against the fence as it passed and brushed against her with its flank. Without a single whinny or snort of complaint from Bittersweet, Jake hooked her to the crossties and patted her neck. He turned a superior gaze on Alison and lifted one corner of his mouth. "A big kick out of watching you?" he repeated. "You've made my day," he chuckled, walking away from them toward a pickup truck that was parked at the end of the stable.

Alison glanced over at Abe, and the little girl looked up, but only briefly. After a few seconds, she went back to combing the doll's hair.

Alison watched Jake walk away, chuckling to himself and crushing his aluminum beer can in his hand. Just then something inside her snapped. She had put up with all she was going to from him. Jake was almost to the truck when her voice behind him halted his steps.

"You are undoubtedly the poorest excuse for a man and for a father I've ever seen."

He spun around, startled.

"I know why you aren't training this horse," she continued, "it's because you don't have the guts to do it. No, you'd rather hide in a drunken stupor." She took a step toward him and tried not to let his

47

size intimidate her. "Wouldn't you?" She reached out and knocked the can from his hand. "I don't know how your daughter manages not to be totally disgusted by you. You certainly disgust me." She wrenched open the door of his truck and glared at him. "So go on, go drink yourself into oblivion. I'm sure your daughter wouldn't know the difference if you were here or not. And I certainly would feel a lot better if you weren't around."

She swiveled and stalked back to the tied horse, stunned by her own outburst. Where had that come from? Where did she get the nerve to yell at a complete stranger like that? What was it about this man that had set her off in the first place? She touched the horse's side and took a deep breath, aware of the stunned silence around her. Neither Abe nor Jake made a sound. All she heard was Bittersweet's steady breathing.

Finally, she heard the crunch of the beer can beneath his boot and the creak of the truck as he climbed up into the driver's seat. "Come on, Abe," he said. "Let's get the hell away from here."

Alison could almost feel the tension between father and daughter, as if it were a cloud that filled the air. She turned around and watched Abe put the doll inside the room, then hesitate, finally reaching for the bicycle that was propped against the wall. She climbed onto it and pedaled in the opposite direction from her father, down the corridor toward the far end of the stable. But her child's voice carried back to them clearly when she said, "I'd rather stay here."

Alison glanced at Jake. His mouth was set, no emotion was visible except for his eyes that watched his daughter ride away from him before he closed the door of the truck and drove away, stirring up the dust in his wake.

Alison picked up the ringing phone, but she immediately clamped her hand over the earpiece so she wouldn't have to listen to that obnoxious rooster recording. It was too early. She had only just gone to sleep, hadn't she? She turned over to hang up the phone, then dropped back to the pillow. Her back was killing her, and her legs felt like lead weights! She'd had no idea how much work one dumb animal could be. Working for as long as she could, she had followed the instructions in the book implicitly, but the day was over before she even got the horse out on the track. After Jake hooked him to the crossties, she cleaned the horse's stall—undoubtedly the most odious task of all—then she pulled the jog cart around and spent the rest of the day trying to figure out how it worked.

She ended the day more tired than she had ever been in her life. Dragging herself back to the motel, she had showered and fallen into bed without even eating any dinner. She couldn't have lifted a fork.

Alison now tossed the covers back, but the effort wore her out. She had to get up. She had to get back out there and get that horse trained if Bittersweet was going to race in July. It was only a month away and Alison had a long, hard course

49

ahead of her, but the biggest hurdle of all seemed to be in making her own legs move off this bed.

She shuffled into the bathroom and began getting ready, this time slipping into the same thing she had worn the day before. Alison McKinsey had never in her life worn an outfit two days in a row, but her yellow blouse and rust-colored slacks were practically ruined from the grit and grime of the stable anyway, and she knew she would never wear them anywhere else. Besides, Jake and Abe wouldn't notice what she had on.

She looked in the mirror above the sink. Staring back at her was not her own image but that of Jake Koske. She saw his eyes the way they had looked yesterday when Abe rode off on her bike. Brown eyes, the color of chocolate, staring out of a face that curtained all emotions. She remembered his hair, tousled and windblown, and the way it had looked when the sun touched it. She also remembered his naked chest, tan and broad, with his hands tucked into the pockets of his faded jeans.

She began to tremble. Something about that man frightened her. There was something untrustworthy about him, as if he were not totally civilized, as if some primal animal lurked inside him. He might turn at any moment, growl, then pounce on her, smothering her with his much stronger body.

Oh, stop it, Alison! The man is a drunken bum. Nothing more, nothing less. The fact that he was able to afford this horse was an amazement in itself, but somehow he had gotten it and now Alison was stuck with both of them. Maybe she could do something about the horse. But the man . . .

Her thoughts flicked to Abe, sitting in the doorway of the tack room, combing her doll's hair. What an odd pair that father and daughter made. What was it that held them together? All he seemed to need her for was to bring him beers or aspirin. Surely the child would rather be living with someone else. And yet . . . an image of that small hand reaching over to lie atop her father's thigh now stuck in her mind. Alison forced her eyes away from the mirror, not wanting to see any more. She didn't want to understand anything but the path in front of her, the one leading back to the life she had left behind in New York.

She slowly walked the length of the barn, in no hurry to resume the physical torture of the day before. Suddenly she stopped short and stared ahead. Bittersweet was bridled and standing in the crossties, and Abe was smoothing a brush along her flank. Abe looked up at Alison, but her expression was cautiously blank. After only a moment, she looked back at the horse and brushed faster and harder.

Alison closed the distance between them. She was always awkward around children, but especially this one. And especially now. "Uh—good morning," she said.

Abe draped an arm around Bittersweet's neck and turned her face into the horse. "Mornin'."

"You've got her ready."

"Yep."

Alison frowned as she reached up absently to stroke the horse's nose. "Why?"

Abe looked up at her, hesitating. "Cause—she's ours. I'm responsible for her."

"How old are you, Abeline?"

"Ten."

Alison was surprised. She seemed much younger—and at the same time much older. "Are you also responsible for your father?"

The little girl lifted her chin defensively. "I take care of him."

"Why? I mean, shouldn't he take care of you? He's the adult—supposedly."

Abe turned her face back to the horse's neck. "He has no one else to take care of him."

"But who takes care of you?" Alison insisted.

Abe, resting her cheek against the neck and smoothing her hand up under the muzzle, narrowed her eyes at the older woman. "You gonna work with Bitty or not?"

Alison mulled over the question for a few seconds. "Are you going to help?"

"Thought I might." She patted Bittersweet's shoulder. "Don't want her hurt."

"Well, then," Alison said with the first hint of a smile toward the girl. "We have something in common. I don't want her hurt either."

CHAPTER FIVE

"The cart needs oil," Abe said, squirting it on a couple of the joints. "She gets jumpy if the jog cart squeaks."

"Why do you have two different types of carts?" Alison asked, holding the bridle while Abe worked on the wheel.

"This is for trainin'. The other one's for racing."

"It says in the book . . ."

Abe looked up, exasperated. "You might as well throw away that dammit book," she said. "I'm gonna teach you everything you need to know."

Alison peered down at the top of that brown, fuzzy head and suppressed a smile over the inaccurate use of one of her father's favorite expletives. Then she thought about what Abe had said about teaching her everything. Never, in all her years, had she ever imagined that a ten-year-old could teach her anything. But then, she had never met the likes of Abeline Elizabeth Koske before either.

Abe stood up and dusted her hands together. "Look," she said, peering up at Alison. "I know the book says you're s'posed to line drive her first and hitch her up slow, but . . . well, she's done all that."

"You mean Jake did train her some?"

Abe shifted nervously and crammed her fists into her front pockets. "Nah. He ain't had time."

Alison regarded her for a long moment, watching her fidget and squirm. "You mean . . . you did it? You've been training her?"

"You aren't gonna tell Jake, are ya?"

A hundred childhood memories were stirred up by the dust Abe scuffed with her foot. Secretive forays down the long, winding hallways, private nooks and crannies in the big Tudor house, mischief-making that was never reported to her father. Alison stared down into those intense brown eyes—miniature replicas of Jake Koske's. She smiled. "No, I won't tell."

Abe suddenly grinned wickedly and moved closer. "She even went in two fifteen for me."

"That means . . ."

"She ran a mile in two minutes, fifteen seconds."

"That's good . . . isn't it?"

"Well, for Bitty, it is. Most of the time I work her out at a slower pace. But I know she can go faster, Ali. I just know it."

Alison couldn't help but be infected by the girl's enthusiasm and optimism. Bittersweet was going to race, and she was going to win. The money was as good as in her pocket.

They spent the rest of the morning working with the horse, going slowly so that Alison could learn how it was supposed to be done. Outside by the track, Abe hooked the shafts of the cart through the tugs on one side while Alison watched and then tried to hook it on the other side. Abe showed her how to climb onto the cart without breaking her leg or having the horse take off at a full trot. She then held the lead reins and Alison, with great misgivings, carefully climbed aboard.

"I don't know about this, Abeline. I just don't . . . ohh!" she screamed as Abe let go of the bridle, handed Alison the reins, and the horse shot out like a cannonball onto the track. "What do I do now!" she screamed back at Abe, who was clutching her stomach, bowled over with laughter.

Alison turned back around, holding fast to the reins with a death grip, as the wind whipped through her hair and slapped against her cheeks. All she could hear was the sound of the horse's hoofs beating against the track, the rhythmic creak of the cart wheels, the rush of the wind against her face, and the terrified pounding of her heart. She was so close to the horse, its tail kept brushing against her foot, and those hooves flying up . . . they were so close . . .

But oh, the exhilaration!

She took a chance of looking up once and saw Abe clapping her hands and jumping up and down. And a few yards down was Jake, one foot propped up on the fence, his arms resting on the top rail, and a look of utter amazement on his face.

All at once feeling cocky, Alison lifted a hand and waved, but he didn't return the gesture. He only stood there and stared.

She wasn't sure how many times she had gone around the track, but as she drew past Abe, she saw her waving and shouting something. Jake had disappeared.

"What?" Alison yelled.

"Slow her down now. Pull her in."

Slow her down. Pull her in. Oh, Lord, how was she supposed to do that. Let's see. You pull on the reins and that was supposed to slow them down. She pulled, but nothing much happened. Bittersweet's adrenaline was obviously pumping and she seemed inclined to go around the track ten times. Alison tugged again, harder this time, and the horse finally began to slow. She pulled once more and the horse began to jog lightly toward the gate. Abe jumped up and reached for the bridle, pulling Bittersweet to a halt.

"I can't believe it!" Alison cried, working her way down from the cart. Her knees were shaky when she finally stood on solid ground. "I can't believe how fast they go."

"I told you Bitty was fast. She could beat every other horse here and not even have to work very hard."

"I believe it. Oh, that was such fun! I can hardly wait until tomorrow."

Abe looked up at her, adoration written in every inch of her smile. "Me neither."

They both stood still for a moment, regarding each other cautiously. Abe turned away first, a high flush coloring her cheeks and the back of her neck. She grabbed hold of the bridle and led Bittersweet into the stable and down the corridor.

"Thank you—for teaching me and letting me do that," Alison ventured to break the silence.

"Why are you here, Ali? I—I mean—why are you doing this with Bitty—you know, working her and stuff?"

They stopped in front of the stall and together they unhooked the shafts of the jog cart from the leather carrier. "I need the money," she answered honestly.

Abe looked her over. "I thought you were rich. You dress in fancy clothes and stuff and—"

"I was rich." She pushed the cart back over and leaned it up against the wall. "I've just had a—a little setback, that's all."

"That's what my dad says he's had, too. A little setback."

Alison glanced over, surprised. She had assumed that Jake Koske was one of those who existed in a permanent state of the down-and-outs.

Abe fastened Bittersweet into the crossties and began unhooking the bridle. She stopped and stared into the horse's neck. "Do you wish you still were rich?"

"Of course," Alison answered, helping to pull the bridle off and hang it up on the hook.

Abe still hadn't moved. She was holding on to the horse and staring at its neck. "If you were rich, you wouldn't be here now, would you?"

Alison came around to the side where Abe was standing. She regarded her closely, wondering why the question was asked and what kind of answer was needed. Finally, she decided that the truth was the only way to deal with this child. "No," she said. "I wouldn't."

Abe nodded slowly, then patted the horse's

shoulder. "Yeah, that's what I figured." She moved away, reaching for a sweat scraper in the trunk and then came back to stroke it down the wet chestnut flanks.

Alison watched Abe minister to the horse, and then she felt another presence in the stall. She turned and looked straight into Jake's eyes and a flash of fear shot through her. He was standing several feet away, but she could tell by the look on his face that he had heard their conversation.

He was watching Alison closely, his mouth held tight, his eyes probing deeply. As usual he was unshaven and held a beer can in his hand, but when he looked at her with those penetrating brown eyes, she felt as if she had been slugged in the midsection. Her breath was gone and she couldn't find it. There was something about him that sent curious quivers of excitement through her. She pulled her eyes away.

He walked up and patted the horse's rump, his eyes now targeted on his daughter as she scraped the sweat off the hide. "So," he said, slowly and thoughtfully, his voice a gentle contradiction to the fire that had emanated from his eyes only a moment ago. "Amazing progress for a horse that hasn't been in training."

The hand holding the scraper stopped and Abe glanced up at him, waiting for a reaction that she was too young to predict. Alison, too, was waiting breathlessly, not knowing what to expect from this unpredictable man.

He draped an arm across the horse's back and

stared intently at the girl. "Why didn't you tell me, Abeline?"

"Tell you what?" Her voice was shaky.

"That you wanted her to race."

"I—dunno. Thought you'd be mad."

"Why?"

She shrugged. " 'Cause—since Mom . . . I don't know. You're mad a lot."

"So you did it when I wasn't around," he said, still watching her closely.

"Yeah, after school. When you—weren't around."

"Guess I haven't been around much at all, have I?"

Abe turned back toward the horse and started scraping. "I dunno. Guess not."

He lifted his hand from his side and reached toward her. She stopped and stared at him, expectant, terrified, hopeful. He almost touched her cheek, he was within inches of her smooth skin. But at the last minute he changed his mind, laying his hand on top of her head and ruffling her hair. His voice when he spoke had a strange catch in it. "You've done a good job, Abe. She's going to be a fine horse."

He raised his eyes to Alison, who had been watching the entire exchange with a pounding heart. Abe was correct when she said he was mad a lot. Alison had noticed it, too, in the short time she'd known him. He always appeared angry at the world; one minute he was ready to smack the first person who got in his way, and in the next he was letting the alcohol carry him into an oblivion where he didn't give a damn about anybody or anything. But he hadn't gotten mad at Abe. Would he now take it out on Alison?

She waited with a tight breath as he set his beer can on the steamer trunk and moved closer, resting his right hand against the wall beside her head. He was too big and overpowering, as if his face and body had been carved from the trunk of a huge oak. Alison tried to swallow.

He bent down, speaking softly, speaking only to her. "So you're broke. I knew it. I could tell." His eyes traveled slowly over her face, cataloguing the soft angles and curves of her features. "If you think you're going to make any money off Bittersweet, I'd suggest you first learn what in the hell you're doing."

The criticism was all it took to stir her up. Overpowering or not, no one got the upper hand with Alison McKinsey. She tilted her head, glaring up at his rough, unshaven face, but she, too, kept her voice low, out of Abe's earshot. "Oh? Is that right? You're a fine one to talk; you're afraid to sober up long enough to work with her."

His jaw flinched, but it was the only sign he had even heard what she was saying. His gaze was sliding down her neck and onto the front of her blouse, then lower still. "That was rather amusing watching you out there on the track," he drawled. "Going round and round in your French designer outfit." He chuckled low in his throat. "A riot, in fact." His face moved closer to hers, hovering only inches above her. "How come you didn't fall off? Huh?"

His nearness was having a debilitating effect on her, but she lifted her chin higher, determined to counteract the unfamiliar sensations he was provoking. She never felt this way around men. She had always been the one in charge. The one with the cutting edge. "You'd like that—wouldn't you?" she snapped.

"Just wondering why, that's all."

"I know what's bothering you. You're jealous."

He sniffed derisively. "What on earth would I be jealous about?"

"Your daughter and I have a common goal. What do you have? Nothing but a bottle of cheap tequila or a six-pack of beer to wallow in."

He straightened up and stepped away, grabbed the can on the trunk, and lifted it in toast to her. "A hot beer, McKinsey. One that needs immediate replacement." He turned and stalked into the tack room, slamming the door behind him.

Alison glanced over at Abe, but the girl continued to stare intently at the horse as the scraper moved rhythmically over its hide.

The next morning was glorious. Alison was surprised she could find anything glorious about this wasteland, but the sky was a pale blue with the flush of early morning still in it, and a flock of birds twittered on the power lines that bordered the road, and she felt terrific.

Abe was sitting on the fence when Alison drove up in her subcompact to the track. Alison waved, stepped out of the car, and strolled over to her.

61

"What do you think?" Abe asked, pointing happily toward the track.

Coming around the far side was a man on a jog cart. Alison recognized the chestnut horse. It was Bittersweet. The man—She did a double take. Good grief! It was Jake! "What brought this on?"

Abe shrugged. "I don't know. I started to ask him but he almost bit my head off. He just got up and came out and hitched her up." Alison sat down beside her on the fence and Abe looked up at her. "He didn't drink anything after you left last night."

Alison's surprised gaze swung back to the track as Jake came around the last curve, moving close to them.

With a scowl on his face, he hollered at them, "You happy now?".

"Ecstatic," Alison hollered back.

Abe was grinning from ear to ear as he went around the track again. "My dad's handsome, isn't he?"

Alison glanced down at her and then lifted her eyes back to the track. She felt that same frightening jolt—the one she felt everytime he came near her. Handsome? All she had seen of Jake Koske was a three-day growth of beard, and a perpetually drunken scowl. She tried to find a diplomatic answer. "Little girls always think their fathers are the most handsome men in the world."

"Did you?"

"Oh, yes." Alison smiled. "My father was so handsome and witty and intelligent."

"Where is he now?"

62

"He died . . . a long time ago."

"How did he die?"

"Heart attack."

"Where's your mom?"

"She died when I was just a baby."

Abe was astounded. "You don't remember her?"

Alison shook her head. "No. I have a picture of her, though. Would you like to see it?"

"Sure."

Alison pulled her purse onto her lap, reached way down into it, and pulled out her billfold. Juggling all the things on her lap, she opened it up and flipped to the photograph of a young woman, fragile and elegant.

Abe closely examined the picture. "She's pretty. You don't look like her."

Sighing, Alison slipped the wallet back into her purse. "Yes, I know."

They were both quiet for a stretch as they watched Jake heading around the track again.

"My mom's pretty too," Abe said, breaking the silence.

"Where is she?"

"She left."

"Left—for where?"

Abe shrugged, staring at the track ahead. "I dunno. With some man."

Alison quickly switched her attention back to Jake as he slowed Bittersweet down and brought her through the gate and into the stable yard. She and Abe jumped off the fence and hurried over to him.

He climbed down from the cart and tossed the

reins to Alison. "That," he declared, "is how you work a pacer."

She pursed her lips and caught the reins. "Most enlightening."

He turned and started walking toward the barn. "She needs a bath," he hollered back.

"So do you," Alison called.

He turned around and stuck his hands in the back pockets of his jeans, his head cocked slightly. "Is that an offer to bathe us both?"

She held on to the horse's bridle and started walking in his direction, revealing an outward calm she did not feel. Just being near him made her flesh run hot and cold, but she wasn't about to let it show. "The horse will be a cinch," she said, brushing past him. "You, on the other hand, are a challenge I'm not quite up to facing."

Jake stood stock-still, watching her wrap her fingers tightly around the reins. He had noticed her hands before—she had slender fingers with perfectly manicured oval nails. She wore a diamond on her right hand and nothing on her left. She might have been one of those liberated married types who preferred the freedom of no wedding ring, but he had called her Miss McKinsey and she hadn't corrected him.

He thought of the way she had looked that first evening when she'd come back to try once again to persuade him to help. He had known her smile and whisper-soft voice were calculated maneuvers to win him over, and she had almost succeeded. He had always been a sucker for beautiful women and this one was more beautiful than most. But this one also spelled trouble with a capital T. He wasn't quite sure why he felt so certain about that; all he knew was that he felt it. Strongly.

Besides, he thought angrily, who the hell was she to come here and start lecturing him about how to live his life or raise his kid? He didn't need anybody to tell him how to do a damn thing, least of all some spoiled, rich broad from the East who looked even more lost in life than he did.

They were well ahead of him when he walked into the barn, furiously scuffing the dirt with his boots as he made his way toward the tack room to pick up a towel, a bar of soap, and some clean clothes. Alison and Abe already had Bittersweet out behind the stable, getting her ready for a bath.

Thirty minutes later, when he came back from the shower room, they were shutting her in the stall and Abe was looping the wire closure on the gate.

Alison turned around and her eyes widened in mute astonishment. At first she didn't recognize the stranger in front of her. This man was closely shaven, clean, and wearing a freshly pressed pair of jeans and shirt. And this man . . . this man was incredibly handsome.

Trying to still the odd little fluttering in her chest, she glanced over at Abe and effected a haughty tone of voice. "Who is this human being? He isn't somebody we know, is he?"

Jake turned surly and walked over to the stall, trying to ignore her sarcasm. He pretended to check out the horse, although with Abe in charge, he knew it wasn't necessary. "She looks adequately clean," he begrudgingly noted.

"Oh, I see." Alison smirked. "You're an expert all of a sudden."

He looked over at her. "That's right."

Abe clambered up on an empty stall gate, swinging it back and forth. "My dad knows everything about animals. He's a veterinarian."

Alison jerked her head toward him, unable to hide her surprise. "A veterinarian?"

"In a former life," he mumbled, turning away.

Alison leaned against the gate to steady herself. This man was full of surprises. "You don't practice now?"

"Does it look like it?"

"It doesn't look to me like you do much of anything."

He nodded. "You've got it."

"Why not?" she prodded.

"You sure do ask a hell of a lot of questions."

"I'm just naturally curious."

"Well, go be curious about someone else."

"What is it about me that you dislike so much?" She let out a slow, uneven breath, cursing herself as a weak fool the moment the words came out of her mouth.

"It's that obvious, is it?"

"Yes."

His gaze was narrowed on her for a long moment, then his eyes slipped down the length of her. She was a beautiful woman, really—interesting looking, with angular features, bright eyes, and auburn hair. But something about her gnawed at him and threw him off-balance. It was the way she carried herself, and the angle at which she held her head, and the tight pinch of her mouth as if she were always bracing herself against some storm at sea. He shook his head. "I don't trust you, that's all."

"Why not?"

"I don't trust you with my horse." He took a step closer, closing the gap between them. He lowered his voice. "And I don't trust you with my daughter."

"Your daughter!" Her return whisper was a hiss. "What damage could I possibly inflict on her that hasn't already been done?"

He bent over, his face menacingly close. "What the hell is that supposed to mean?"

"A ten-year-old girl living in a tack room with her alcoholic father, deserted by her mother for some other man . . ."

His eyes darted to his daughter, but she had moved farther down to another gate and was climbing around, paying no attention to the furious whispers several yards away. "What has she told you?" he snapped.

"Enough to know that life has been anything but fair to her."

He sniffed. "Nobody said life was supposed to be fair. If I can teach her that, I've done my job."

"If you do that, you've done less than a tenth of your job."

"Oh, so now you're an expert on raising kids, huh?"

She stared up at him, her cool gray eyes battling

the brown glare he was pinning her with. "I don't know a thing about kids. All I know is what it's like to be a little girl without a mother and with a father who is so wrapped up in his own life and troubles that he doesn't have time to see what his growing daughter needs. That, I do know."

When she had finished speaking, he looked into her eyes. There was a wetness in them now that softened the color. Not tears exactly, but—feeling. He had a hunch she didn't do that very often, and he didn't like the tug it caused in the pit of his stomach.

Abe came skipping back up and started to get on her bike. Jake turned toward her, wanting to push Alison's problems aside. They were her problems. He had enough of his own to worry about. He didn't need hers to lug around. "Abe, you've got to get cleaned up if you're going with me tonight."

"Oh, Dad," she cried excitedly. "Can Ali go with us to eat?"

"Who in tarnation is Ali?"

Mentally kicking herself for having let any emotions show a moment before, Alison picked up her purse from atop the trunk and swung it jauntily over her shoulder. "I am."

"Oh," he grumbled. "Should have known." He looked back and forth between the two of them and shrugged. "Suit yourself."

Alison smiled at Abe. "Thanks anyway, but I'd better not."

"We're going to Eddie's," Abe eagerly insisted. "Dad'll play cards and I won't have anybody to—"

68

Jake laid his hand on top of her head. "Forget it, Abe. She thinks she's too good for us. Come on, let's get ready."

Alison stiffened her spine and stepped between them, elbowing Jake aside. "I most certainly do not think such a thing. And I'd love to go. What time?"

The heat from Jake's glare could have soldered iron. Damn, but she would ruin his evening. "Soon as she's cleaned up," he muttered, wishing Abe would stop that excited jumping up and down beside him. "We'll pick you up at the motel."

Alison's smile was triumphant. "Wonderful."

CHAPTER SIX

Jake's gaze lingered on the western sky. It was that time between day and night, after the red band of sunset had faded away, but before the shadow of night had fully arched over the sky. A quiet time. Usually a peaceful time. But not tonight. Instead, he was tapping his hand impatiently against the steering wheel of his truck and cursing to himself. What in hell was taking them so damn long!

He was parked on the gravel lot of the Island in the Sun Motel, just outside her door. Number seven. He had sent Abe to get her, but he hadn't expected her to go inside and close the door. Now the two of them were holed up in there together like a couple of jack rabbits and he was stuck out here—waiting by himself. Abe's behavior this evening had been really strange. Instead of just throwing something on, as she usually did when they went somewhere, she had gone into a tizzy over what to wear. Her drawers were turned upside down and every article of clothing she owned was dumped on both of their beds. She was acting like some typically crazy female and that just wasn't Abe.

He slapped the wheel again. What were they doing in there! Abe was the one who wanted Alison McKinsey tagging along anyway; it certainly wasn't him. He didn't even like her. There was something about that woman that set his teeth on edge. *"Why do you dislike me so much?"* She had a low voice for a woman. Soft, too. The memory of it stirred down deep in his abdomen. Maybe that was part of the reason he didn't like her. She made him think of her in a way he didn't want to. There were enough women around this town to ease his sexual urges anytime he wanted. He certainly didn't need some desperate heiress from New York City screwing up his life. It was already screwed up enough.

He rested his elbow in the open window and noticed the first star of the evening. Star light, star bright, first star I see . . .

It had been an evening—much like this one. Abe had been lying down in the front yard of their two-story Victorian, gazing up at the gathering night, quoting the familiar nursery rhyme. He had been sitting on the porch railing, staring at the front door. The screen door swung open and a flurry of long blond hair, tight jeans, and a red silk blouse rushed past him and down the steps. "Where are you going?" he had asked.

"Out," she'd replied curtly. The car door opened and she climbed in behind the wheel of the black Porsche.

"When will you be home, MaryAnn?"

"Later."

When the car disappeared down the street, he

71

had glanced over at his daughter. She was sitting up in the grass, her eyes following the curve of the street, as if by staring hard enough she alone could end her mother's mysterious errands and secretive missions that came at all hours of the day and night. Jake was more realistic. He knew that his marriage was about to end.

He pulled his eyes away from the star and glared at door number seven. Two more minutes and then he was leaving, and they could walk to the restaurant.

Before the threat could take shape, the door opened and they walked out. For a moment, he was stunned. He saw Abe first. Her hair was slicked back on one side and held by a gold barrette. They had gone together to the movies last month and the starring girl had worn her hair the same way. He stared a moment longer and then his eyes shifted to Alison. She was wearing a pair of brushed-denim jeans, soft and snug, and a turquoise silk blouse with matching shoes. Her hair, too, was brushed back on one side and held with a clip. He was aware of a pounding inside his chest, but he didn't realize he was staring until Abe grinned and asked, "How do we look?"

Almost mechanically, he jumped out of the truck and came around to open the door for them. "Great, honey," he mumbled distractedly, but his eyes were still on Alison. "You, uh, look, uh . . . You went to a lot of trouble for Eddie's."

Abe climbed into the truck first, and Alison reached for the door handle to pull herself up. She looked up at Jake. "I didn't do it for Eddie's. . . ."

A pulse began to pound in his head and he waited with a kind of adolescent breathlessness that he thought he had lost twenty-five years ago.

She cocked her head and smiled playfully. "I did it for me."

"Should have known," he grumbled as she climbed in and he slammed the door behind her. He walked around to his side, cursing his overly excited hormones and vowing not to let her affect him in any way. He started the motor and the truck squealed out of the parking lot like a bat out of hell.

They drove in silence down Main Street and searched for a place to park the truck. It was one of those nights when everybody—but everybody, was heading for Eddie's Bar and Grill. The music from the jukebox spilled out into the street and carried all the way to the end of the block.

"What are you gonna do about the motel, Ali?" Abe asked as Jake swung the truck around in the middle of the street, heading back for a spot he had found.

Alison blushed and quickly shook her head. "Oh . . . it's . . . I'll worry about it later."

"Worry about what?" Jake asked, throwing the truck into reverse to back into the space. "What's the problem with the motel?"

"Oh, it's nothing. . . ."

Abe thought differently. "The owner told her she had to pay up for the full week if she was gonna stay any longer. She's a mean old goat," she added. "I don't like her."

"It's really nothing," Alison said, blushing even

73

more as Jake fixed his stare on her. "I'll take care of it. Really."

But Abe had it all figured out. "What you need is a regular place to stay. For good. Not some dumb old motel. Who wants to live in a place like that anyway?"

"Yes," Alison mumbled, trying to ignore Jake's penetrating brown-eyed stare. "I may try to look around for something a little—"

"Cheaper?" he asked, his voice flat and dry, his eyes piercing through her.

She sighed. "Yes."

He turned off the motor and rested his arms on the wheel, staring straight ahead, wishing the subject had never come up, wishing he could just go to Eddie's, have a few beers, play some cards, and maybe slide a woman's soft body up against him for a couple of dances. Wishing he didn't care. After a minute, he turned toward her again. "There's an empty tack room at the stable," he said, his voice still flat with that curious lack of commitment.

Involuntarily, she shuddered at the idea of living in a filthy barn.

"She could move in with us!" Abe cried, filled with a child's ebullience over finding so perfect a solution to the problem. "We can put in another cot. Wouldn't it be fun?"

Jake and Alison were looking at each other, and she felt the color rising up her neck and cheeks. "I don't think so," Jake said, his eyes never leaving Alison's face. "That's just not . . ."

Alison tore her eyes away from him and looked

74

down at Abe. "It wouldn't be proper," she informed her with a tone of formality.

"Why? When I've slept over with a friend, Jake's had other ladies sleep in there."

His face paled. Dammit! he thought, and then hurriedly opened the door of the truck and stepped out, letting the night air brush over him and whisk away his discomposure. It didn't help much. He walked around and opened Alison's door, but he wouldn't look at her. He didn't have to. He knew that right now her eyes were drilling a cold, gray hole through him.

"Heard you was out running that filly of yours s'mornin'," one of the men commented, tipping his mug back to drain the last of the beer. They had pushed several tables together and were sitting with ten other people.

"That's right." Jake nodded.

"You ain't planning on staking her, are you?"

"Thought I might."

A round of laughter followed, and one of the women leaned closer and placed her hand on his arm. "Jake, honey, how are you going to get her legged up in time? I thought you were gonna let her idle for a year, then race her as a three-year-old."

He glanced over at Alison and lifted his mug to his lips. "That was before my partner came to town."

It looked to him as if Alison was trying desperately not to squirm beneath the speculative stares. She smiled bravely. "We—uh—we think she is going to do really well in the races." She glanced down at Abe for support. "Don't we?"

Abe rose to the occasion, grinning from ear to ear. "Anybody want to start laying odds on her?"

An indulgent chuckle was passed around the table. "Boy, if she ain't a chip off the old block . . ." Someone laughed. "But, no siree, I'll believe this bit of action when I see it with my own two eyes. Hey, how come you two end up with a partner anyhow? I thought you won that filly in a card game."

Jake's gaze shot to Alison. She was staring with wide eyes at him. "I did," he said slowly, letting his eyes swing back to the group. "But I only won Ed Hopkins's half. He had a partner." He didn't look back at her, but he could feel the heat from her eyes upon him. He had assumed she'd known who the original partner was, but, from the surprise on her face, she apparently had not. He mentally marked it down as another strike against her. What kind of woman didn't even know what she owned or who owned it with her? Where had her head been all these years?

The waitress brought their cheeseburgers and several baskets of fries and Abe ordered another Coke. She was in high spirits and Jake knew why. Abe's eyes kept dancing up to Alison sitting next to her, and the two of them kept putting their heads together to whisper conspiratorially. He couldn't miss the blatant worship that shone in Abe's eyes every time she looked at Alison, and that worried him. Ms. McKinsey would hang around long enough to get Abe and him to help her train and race Bittersweet. Then she planned on selling the horse. After she got what she had come for, she'd hightail it back to New York City and Abe would be left behind all over again. Regardless of what he had said to Alison about life not being fair, he wasn't going to let his little girl be hurt again.

Alison hadn't decided what was bothering her the most about her big night out at Eddie's—the smoke in the bar that was so thick you could cut it with a knife, the blaring whine of country music, the raucous laughter and jokes in which she was not invited to take part, or simply the fact that Jake Koske fit in whereas she did not.

So, until she heard the talk turn to horses, she kept her conversation directed to Abe. She glanced around the room, wondering again what she was doing here. She wanted to have fun, she really did. But . . . well, it was all so different from the type of restaurant or bar she usually went to, and she seemed to have nothing in common with any of these people.

Jake was leaning back in his chair, his arms folded across his chest, his eyes roaming over the room. He looked so different since he had shaved and changed into freshly pressed clothes that she could hardly believe he was the same man. His hair was a little long, but neatly styled, and it was thick and brown and looked as if it would be very soft to touch. His jaw was firm and, when he smiled, he had a very nice mouth. But sometimes when he looked at her, there was a wild light in his eyes, something bright that burned through her skin, igniting all of her senses. He caught her staring and she blushed, but in the low light she hoped he had been unable to tell. Resting her elbows on the table, she clasped her hands beneath her chin. "You didn't tell me you won the horse in a card game."

"Figured you already knew."

"Who is Ed Hopkins?"

"The man who owned half of Bittersweet before me."

"So he was my original partner, I guess."

"I guess so. Seems kind of odd you didn't know him."

His tone was almost accusing, which brought a defensiveness to her answer. "A firm in New York handled all of my investments. I didn't get involved."

"Obviously."

"Well," she retorted. "Maybe this Ed Hopkins would have trained her long before now."

"Yeah, and maybe he would have killed her."

Alison jumped at the unexpected tone in his voice. "What makes you say that?"

Abe's eyes began to flash, and it was she who answered. "He was mean to Bitty," she snapped. "He's mean to everything and everybody."

Alison looked back to Jake for confirmation. He nodded. "Bittersweet was in pretty bad shape when I took her. She was undernourished, she hadn't been washed for who knows how long, she had the wrong shoes on her feet, and she even had a couple of open sores on her legs. I didn't think she would ever race when I first saw her."

78

"Is that why you haven't trained her much be-fore now?"

"Part of the reason. She needed a rest. Of course, the other reason is that you didn't pay me."

"I didn't know anything about that," she argued.

He just shrugged. "It was your money. You were ultimately responsible. You know, the sooner you learn that, the better off you'll be."

"Well, well," she snipped. "Listen to Mr. Paragon of Responsibility himself."

He leaned forward, his face rock hard as he glared at her. "Listen, lady, my life may be a mess right now, but at least I'm not blaming somebody else for causing it. I take full responsibility for everything that's happened. That's what separates adults from children. So maybe you ought to grow up and do the same."

Her own face had grown brittle with each truthful word he uttered. But through her own indignation at him, something else surfaced. It was the realization that he wasn't angry at the world the way she had supposed. His anger was all directed at himself.

The couples who were dancing came back to the table, and to Alison's acute relief the conversation shifted to include everyone. The men moved down to Jake's end of the table and started playing poker. After a while Abe folded her arms on the table and laid her head down on them, closing her eyes. Alison glanced at the gold Rolex on her wrist. It was ten-thirty, well past any kid's bedtime. She glanced over at Jake, but he was laughing with the other men and having a great time, not in the least inclined to pack up and go. In fact, it looked as if he were winning the game.

She reached over and started to touch his arm, but decided against it. Instead, she spoke a little louder. "Listen, Jake, why don't I take Abeline back to the motel with me. She can sleep there and you won't have to worry about her." As if he were worrying about her now, she thought irritably.

His eyes flicked to his sleeping daughter, her head cradled on her arms, the gold barrette barely hanging to a thin strand of hair. He looked back at Alison. "I can go now too."

"No," she insisted too sharply. "You—you stay and have a good time. We'll just take your truck, if that's okay."

His eyes were centered on her face, his expression unreadable. "It's okay," he said evenly. "But I could come with you."

She reached for her purse under the table and stood up, bending over Abe to wake her up. "It's not necessary." Oh, who are you kidding, Alison. It was more than unnecessary. It would be disastrous! Maybe it was the beer she'd drunk. Maybe that was why she now had these restless feelings inside her, but she didn't really believe that. She knew it was the way he looked tonight, the way he smiled and laughed and spoke in that low, easy voice. It was his hands and his eyes and his broad shoulders. It was him. And all she wanted right now was to get away from him as quickly as possible.

"Abeline," she whispered. "It's time to go."

Abe rubbed her eyes and stood up, swaying against Alison's body as she was led out the door. Jake held his cards loosely in his hands as he watched them go, his gaze centered on the snug fit of Alison's jeans across her hips, the rhythm of her walk, the arm around his daughter, and the bright trail of color she left in her wake. Still watching her, he laid his cards on the table, mumbling, "Gin."

The other men at the table stopped and gawked at him as if he had suddenly gone daft. "That's great, Jake," one of them laughed. "The only problem is we're playing five-card stud."

Alison jumped at the knock on the door and set her book down on the table by the bed. But it was several seconds before she could calm the racing of her pulse enough to stand up and walk across the room. When she opened the door, Jake swayed slightly and his lopsided grin told her he was more than a little tipsy.

She tried to look stern, but it was a poor attempt. "Well?" she asked, resting her hands on her waist.

"Well what?"

"Did you win?"

He frowned, thinking, and then crammed his hands deep into his pockets. He pulled them out, wrong side out, and then lifted his sheepish eyes to her face. "I guess not." He craned around her to see his daughter sleeping on the bed. "Guess I'd better take the kid home now."

"Why don't you just leave her for the night. I'll bring her with me in the morning."

He scowled, but in his drunken state the expression looked more comical than sinister. "You don't think I'm responsible enough to take care of her, do you?"

"I didn't say a word."

"But you think it, don't you?"

She sighed, rapidly losing her patience with him. Why was it that she had only to be around him for five minutes before he started getting on her nerves? "Look, Jake, I just thought it would give you a chance to do whatever you want without a kid hanging around. The tack room will be empty."

"What is that supposed to mean?" he snapped, grabbing the door frame to keep his balance.

"Nothing," she snapped back. "I just thought you'd like the freedom to take someone home with you."

His eyes darkened and his scowl deepened. "I hadn't planned on taking anyone back with me."

She shrugged, trying a little too hard for a complacency she wanted desperately to feel, but did not. "Suit yourself."

"Believe me," he growled. "I will."

They both stood in the doorway, no more than a foot apart, with a sleeping child on one side and the dark, moonless night on the other. Neither spoke for several long seconds as the tension swelled around them. Finally, he lifted his eyes

82

from the ground and narrowed them on her face. "You didn't have much fun tonight, did you?"

His voice still wasn't friendly, but it had lost that low, ominous growl.

"It was fine," she answered.

"No, it wasn't. Don't lie. You hated it. We're not your kind of people." She started to speak, but he rushed on before she could. "We don't have the class you're used to, isn't that right?"

"Don't be absurd," she said, flustered because she didn't have a good answer for him. They weren't her kind of people. But she didn't know why. "It had nothing to do with that," she murmured noncommittally.

"Oh, I saw you," he said in an accusing tone. "You were sitting there all night with your nose up in the air, and with that supercilious gleam in your eye."

"That's not true!" She glared at him, but the more intense heat blazing from his eyes made her look away. "I—I just didn't feel that I belonged. You're all friends. No one—talked to me or—or included me."

"How could they when you had that nose stuck up in the air so high?" He took a step forward, angling toward her, and she edged out the door to escape him. But it only moved her into the shadows against the wall where he could trap her. "You have this look about you," he murmured, low and huskily. "A look that says do not touch, keep off the grass, keep away. No one would dare get near you. Some alarm might go off, or they might get twenty to life for just looking at you the wrong way."

83

She wished he would move away from her. "I'm very well liked in my circle of friends," she whispered defensively.

"Well, I sure as hell hope I never have to meet any of your friends, then."

"They say I'm fun," she retorted. "And witty, and . . . and attractive." She stopped when she realized how he was staring at her. It was different this time, more purposeful, more powerful, more intimate. He propped his hands against the wall on each side of her head.

His eyes moved from her forehead down her face and dropped lower to the narrow space that existed between them. He lifted his gaze slowly back up to her mouth, where it stopped. "Yes," he said, breathing huskily, lowering his head. "You are that. You are definitely attractive."

Her eyes were wide open as she watched him drawing near, his mouth lowering over hers. You are crazy, Alison. You should push him away. Immediately. Tell him no. You don't want this. But when his lips finally closed over hers, she realized with the quickening inside her that she did not want to push him away. Her mouth moved with his, giving him all the encouragement he needed. His hands lowered to her shoulders, sliding down her arms. With his hands, he lifted hers to his chest and they slid naturally up over his shoulders and around his neck, clinging. Her lips parted and he deepened the kiss, filling her. This was different from the other kisses she had known. He was different from the other men she had been with. This consumed her in a frightening and exhilarating way.

It was all too soon when he released his hold and pulled back, but his face was still very close as he looked down at her. She could see his chest rising and falling unevenly, and his breath was quick and shallow. "You'll take care of my little girl for me, won't you?"

The sound of his voice sent another shiver of longing through her and she nodded weakly, unable to find the breath to speak. When he walked away, she leaned back against the wall, drained and weak. The irony of how much her life had changed and how far she had come from all she knew did not hit her at this moment. The last man she had kissed had been in black tie and drove off in a Mercedes back to his country estate. She didn't remember him. All she was aware of was that Jake's mouth and arms had made her feel more alive than she had ever felt, as if his primal force had been transferred to her and was now running full and strong through her body. Her eyes were still searching the cloud of dust that he had left behind long after he drove away into the night.

CHAPTER SEVEN

The morning was bright, with a few high cirrus clouds sliding gracefully across the sky like skaters on ice. A warm breeze blew over the track, ruffling Alison's hair and lifting it off the back of her neck. She was sitting on the jog cart next to Jake, and her forehead was creased with tiny lines as she concentrated hard on what he was trying to teach her.

"Light hands, Alison. That's the key."

She shook her head and glanced off in the distance at Abe, perched on the white fence watching them. "I don't understand."

He took a deep breath. Patience had never been his strong suit, at least that's what everyone always told him. But he was trying. "It's a feeling, uh . . . here, let me see if I can show you. You won't ever be driving her in any races, of course, but it might help if you understand what we're doing."

She watched him move, felt the cart dip as he shifted his body until his chest was braced against her back, his legs on either side of hers, his arms reaching around from behind to grasp her hands. Her heart began to beat quickly and her hands grew clammy in his grip. He wrapped her fingers over the reins and laid his over them.

"See," he said, his breath rustling the hair behind her ear. "Your tendency is to grip them. But look, loosen up a bit. Light, see?"

She could almost hear the pounding of her heart, and she was sure he could hear it too. The sound of it moved from her chest, up her neck, and into her ears, and her body tightened with the tension that his nearness created. She could feel his breath against her shoulder, and she didn't think she could move. Ever. But when his fingers stroked slowly over the backs of her palms and up her arms, she jerked her hands away from the reins, pulling them back into the fold of her lap. "Yes," she said, her voice sounding jerky and unnaturally high. "I see. Light."

He expelled his breath slowly and shifted back to the side of her, his eyes trained on her profile. "Anyway," he said, clearing his throat. "You get the idea now . . . I guess."

She finally turned toward him, intent on proving to him and to herself that she was there for one purpose only, and that she had no interest in pursuing anything personal with him. "Could she win any races, Jake?"

He nodded slowly. "She could. She's very fast. And she comes from a long line of winners."

Alison's eyes grew brighter and her voice was now crisp and light with purpose. "If she wins a bunch of races, how much do you think we could get for her?"

He glanced out over the field beyond the track,

his thoughts on her question. "I don't know," he finally mumbled, still staring out into the horizon.

"Approximately," she urged. "That's all I want, just an approximate figure."

He turned back to her. "Maybe we won't want to sell her."

"What! What on earth are you talking about? Of course we will. That's the whole idea."

His mouth had drawn out to a hard thin line. "For you it is."

Alison shook her head, confused by the turn of this conversation. After all, that was what they had been working for, wasn't it? "What—what would you do with her if you kept her?"

His expression was unchanging, his eyes fixed, his mouth pulled tight. "Breed her," he said in a slow, controlled voice.

"I don't understand."

With a heavy sigh, his face turned back toward the fields to the east. "I want to start a breeding farm. It's what I've always wanted." All of a sudden, he was self-conscious, deciding he had revealed too much, given a piece of himself to her without a hint as to what she would do with that part of him. He looked back at her, his eyes cautiously blank. "She'd make an excellent mare, Alison. She's got great blood."

"I want to sell her, Jake. That's why I'm here. If you want to keep her, why don't you buy my half from me?"

"I don't have the money."

"I have to sell her," she insisted. "That is why I

88

came here. That's why I'm going through all of this —this . . ."

His face hardened, resembling a chunk of granite. "Oh, I'm well aware of why you are here." He silently cursed himself for telling her about his dream for the future. Why had he let go of any part of himself? He should have known she would toss it aside as if it were of no consequence. This woman was interested in one thing only. Alison McKinsey. He was a fool to feel the way he did around her. He had let her crawl beneath his skin and work her way into his every thought and desire. But no more. As she had made perfectly clear, she would use anyone to get what she wanted. He'd be damned if it was going to be him . . . or his kid.

He picked up the reins and turned the horse straight along the track, then pulled the cart to a halt. "Lesson's over, McKinsey. I've got a horse to work."

Alison slowly and carefully climbed down off the cart and stared in bewilderment as Jake snapped the reins and took off, scattering a cloud of dust over her as he left her behind. What had she said? What had she done to make him so angry? The man was totally irrational, that was his problem. A breeding farm. How ridiculous! Well, it was obvious he had just never grown up and she was simply going to have to be the stronger of the two. She would be the one to keep him on track—her track, the one that would lead to money in the bank and a return to the life she wanted.

"What d' ya think, Ali? Isn't it great!"

Alison stood in the doorway of the vacant tack room, with the afternoon light in the stable corridor at her back, and tried to find the words that would hide what she really thought about this dusty, cramped, worm-eaten hole that she was supposed to call her temporary home. Abe was waiting for her enthusiastic reply, and the longer she hesitated, the farther away the words drifted. "It's, uh, well, it's—gee, I hardly know what to say."

"That's a switch," the male voice behind her taunted, making her spin toward him. "You've been pretty blunt the whole time you've been here so far," Jake retorted with a disagreeable tone, still angry over her refusal this morning to listen to his idea about the breeding farm. "Why try to be diplomatic now? Abe's old enough to understand that you find this whole way of life deplorable, that you're too damn fancy to live in a stable, that you're too damn good to get your hands dirty, that . . ."

"That's enough," she snapped, stepping out of the doorway and standing before him, her hands on her hips. "I've had it with you. I've had it with your criticism of me. You have no idea what I think, Jake Koske. You know nothing about me. You have the audacity to call me a snob, but you—you are one of the biggest snobs I've ever seen. You say I can't stand living this way, but what you're really thinking is that I don't have what it takes. I'm not tough like you. I don't have any grit. That's it, isn't it?" She stepped closer, tilting her

90

head up and glaring into those steady brown eyes. "You know what I think?" she whispered, her voice as cold as ice. "I think you're afraid that maybe I can make it. That maybe I can turn this— this filthy pesthole of a room into a home. And then Mr. Macho Jake Koske won't look quite so macho anymore. That's it, isn't it?"

"Lady," he sneered, "you won't last a week in this room. I can guarantee it."

"Well, well." She smiled imperiously. "Jake Koske the gambling man. I think I feel a wager coming on."

"You've got yourself a bet, lady. You name the stakes."

So sure of himself. So cocky that he was right, that she wouldn't last a week. Well, she'd show him. "Your training fees," she said.

The poker face started to crumple as suspicion crept in. "What about them?"

"If I win, I don't owe you any back pay for training. Only from the day you started training after I got here." She smirked at him. "What's the matter, Koske? Lose your nerve?"

He hesitated, but only for a moment while his own confidence resurfaced. "You're on, McKinsey."

She watched him spin on the heels of his boots and stalk away. She then turned and noticed Abe sitting on the side of the bare cot, her elbow propped on her knee, her chin cupped in her palm, her face as inscrutable as the best deadpan poker player's ever was. And Alison wondered what cards she held in those small hands of hers.

Whatever they were, Alison knew that the stakes for Abe were higher than any she and Jake might come up with.

Alison lifted her gaze to the dark, dusty room and wondered what had possessed her to make a bet like that with Jake. Suddenly she was not only unsure of whether she could make it for one whole week in there. She was wondering if she could make it through one whole night.

"Well," Abe said, standing up and looping her thumbs in her suspenders. "I reckon we'd better get started."

With one final sigh, Alison nodded and together they began to transform the empty tack room into a home.

Through the remainder of the afternoon, they cleaned up the room. And while Jake worked Bittersweet the next morning, Abe and Alison went shopping in town. They bought some inexpensive cotton curtains and a bedspread at Woolworth's, a bucket of paint at the hardware store, and a four-drawer chest at Alison's first—and she hoped last —garage sale. After lunch at the Tastee-Freeze, they came back and painted every surface in the room. The shelves, the floor, the walls, the ceiling, the chest of drawers, the wooden countertop— everything was now shiny and clean with the new coat of paint.

"You're really good at this, Ali. Your house in New York must be really neat. Did you fix it up too?"

Alison finished hooking up the print curtains

and turned around. "Well, I had some help, but I did a lot of the planning."

. "What is it like?" Abe was sitting in the middle of the rollaway bed, now draped with a bright bedspread that was covered in red and yellow flowers.

She sat down beside Abe on the bed, and compared this stable closet with memories of her spacious and elegant town house. "Well, I have—had a lot of this color in the house."

"My mom's favorite color was blue. She had lots of blue dresses and shorts and stuff. She's real pretty and Dad always said she looked good in blue."

"That's nice," Alison mumbled, thinking grimly that it was anything but nice. She did not particularly want to hear anything about Jake's wife.

"Yeah," Abe continued, oblivious of the havoc she was stirring up in Alison's mind. "Everybody thinks so. Dad used to tell her she was prettier than a peach." Her eyes dropped to the bedspread. "That was when I was just a little kid, but I 'member it, though."

Alison stared down thoughtfully at the girl beside her, aware for the first time that Abe was something more than just a kid who was sometimes cute and at other times simply underfoot. She was a human being with feelings of her own. "You miss your mother, don't you?"

Abe traced her finger around one of the red flowers on the bedspread. "I dunno. I guess sometimes."

"Do you ever get to talk to her or—or see her?"

"Nah. I figure she's sore at me about something, but my Dad says it ain't me, it's him. He says she got mad at him. That's why she went away. But I don't know. He might be wrong." She glanced up, her mind catching on a brighter thought. "We had a real neat house in Quincy. It was real big and white and we had a real big porch that went all the way around."

"It sounds great," she said, drawn instantly closer to this girl who was both very young and insecure and also mature beyond her years. In one moment, she was a child, with a child's doll and thoughts and curiosity. And in the next, she was too grown up, forced to accept circumstances that were unfair to a child. Alison realized with a start that she was going to miss Abe very much when she went back to New York.

She tried not to dwell on it, so she thought instead about the information Abe provided her about their previous life. She found it so hard to imagine Jake Koske in a big white house, working as a veterinarian, married to a pretty wife. She felt a sharp wrenching in her stomach as she recalled Abe's words. *He used to tell her she was prettier than a peach.* She tried to get rid of the feeling in the pit of her stomach, but it wouldn't go away. She wasn't even sure why she felt it. It didn't matter to her what Jake had said to his wife. It didn't matter in the least.

"Do you like my dad?"

Alison jumped at the question, standing up quickly and picking up the bundle of orange flowers she had picked beside the road. She began arranging them in the empty paint bucket. "Well," she stammered. "Of—of course. I mean, we have our differences of opinion and all, but he seems like a—a reasonably nice—"

"No," Abe interrupted impatiently. "I mean like a boyfriend. Don't you think he's kinda neat . . . ya know, handsome and all? Most ladies do. A bunch of ladies are always trying to talk to him and dance with him and stuff. None of 'em are as pretty as you. Oh, hi, Dad."

Jake was standing in the doorway, half in the dusty haze of the stable corridor, half in the glow of the newly painted room. And his steady brown eyes were riveted on her face. She knew, in that moment, that he saw what she had been trying to deny to herself for days. He saw the desire that she felt for him. She didn't want it to be there, but she couldn't help herself. Those feelings would not go away. And now he would not go away either.

Jake stood there, not wanting to feel anything for this woman; he didn't want this tide of primal cravings rushing over him everytime he looked at her. It was there every time he laid eyes on that mass of red hair, those cool gray eyes, that slim figure beneath the haute couture. They didn't agree on anything, not the horse, or Abe, or his friends, or their different life-styles. Not a damn thing. Besides that, she wasn't going to hang around here. As soon as she got what she came for, she'd pack up and be long gone. This wasn't a place she would very likely come back to.

"Looks like we're neighbors," he heard her say, in a slightly tremulous voice.

"Looks that way," he answered, making sure his tone was noncommittal.

"So," she murmured, wanting desperately to look away or look nonchalant or . . . or anything but the way she must look right now. "If you want to borrow a cup of sugar or . . ." Her voice trailed off when she saw Jake glance at Abe.

The little girl, understanding some silent cue, climbed off the bed and stepped around her father, jumped down onto the dirt floor of the stable, and wandered out of sight. Jake moved into the room and closed the door behind him, never taking his eyes off Alison. He took two long strides and was in front of her.

"Or what?" he asked, his voice low and gravelly.

She shook her head from side to side as her thoughts began to swim around in her brain. "I don't know." She swallowed. "I just meant—"

In one smooth motion he reached for her and pulled her to him, closing his arms around her body as his mouth fastened over hers. Her pulse thundered in her ears at the uncontained urgency in his kiss. She didn't want him to do this, she tried to convince herself. But in her heart she wanted it to go on and on forever.

When he finally tore his mouth away and grazed a path across her cheek to her ear, she tried to find the breath to speak. "Jake, I don't think we should . . . I don't want to—"

"Neither do I," he groaned, crushing her lips beneath his mouth once again. "Neither do I," he insisted again, this time forming the words against her parted lips. His hand slid around her waist, his fingers digging into the flesh at her sides. Her own arms were entwined around his neck, giving him easy passage to move his hand between them, lifting upward to cover her breast.

No! her mind screamed. You are wrong for me. This is wrong for me. I don't want to get involved with you. But it's only temporary, her senses argued. Go with it. You've never felt like this before, never felt this alive, so let him go, let him make you feel it.

His fingers fumbled with the top button of her blouse, loosening it and moving down to the next. There was an urgency about him that no other man had had with her, a burning need in him that frightened her. But she couldn't pull away from it. It consumed her, making her only want more and more. When his mouth moved away the second time, it was she who moaned until he came back, assuaging the need that was growing with every passing second.

He smelled of the sun and the horse and the fields around them, and his arms were strong and warm and very sure.

Her blouse was open and his fingers roamed across her skin, burning a path with each touch. He was so much more a man than those she had known in the past. She felt her head drop back into the cup of his large hand and she knew he was looking down into her face. But she kept her eyes closed, loving the feel of his fingers as they unfastened the front clasp on her bra and moved onto her breast, stroking her flesh. When he touched her this way, colors seemed to appear magically.

The brilliant colors of her world were within reach, they floated all around her.

He wrapped his arms tightly around her, his mouth moving in a smooth caress over her hair. "How am I going to sleep next door, knowing you're here?" he groaned, holding her even tighter. "If it weren't for Abe . . ."

He left the sentence unfinished. There was no need to say it, for they both knew it all too clearly. A little girl was on the other side of this door, a young, confused, but expectant child wanting her world to be perfect and right and good, but not having the faintest idea what would make it so. They had to be careful with her. They both knew that whatever it was between them was only physical, and they had to make sure that they did not fill Abe with the wrong expectations. They had to be careful—with her and with each other.

Alison's breath was irregular as she leaned into Jake's chest, willing her body to regain its control. She wanted to stay like this—in the warmth of his arms, her head against his chest—forever.

He pulled back, holding her out in front of him, and his eyes swept over her face. "I didn't want to get involved with you, Alison. I don't need you in my life right now."

She nodded and reached up to fasten her bra. She began trying to button her shirt, but her fingers were shaking too badly. "I'm here for only one thing, Jake," she asserted, wanting as much as he did to end this madness before it got out of hand. "I'm here to make money on the horse, and then I'll leave. I have to get this money. That's all I want."

He regarded her closely. "I know that. And—I'll try to help you get it. For both of our sakes—and for Abe's—I think the sooner we sell Bittersweet, the better it will be."

"Yes."

He turned away and stepped toward the door, his hand reaching out for the knob. But he turned back at the last minute before opening it. "I just want you to know that I'm going to try not to let this happen again. I'm going to try very hard." He hesitated, as if he wanted to say more, but his attention shifted to the tiny room around them. "Red?" he marveled, aware for the first time what she had done. He was stupefied. "You're actually going to live in a room that is bright red?"

Her heart was still pounding from his touch, and she had trouble switching to the new topic. "I need color. Everything here is so . . . so . . . brown."

He stared at her for a long moment before responding. "Yeah, well, we kinda like it that way." With that, he stepped down into the stable and closed the door behind him, leaving her alone with a flushed face and a crimson room.

CHAPTER EIGHT

Alison slugged her pillow again and turned over, the sleepless cycle repeating itself once more. She had stopped reaching for her watch on the shelf, not wanting to see that minute hand creep laboriously around the dial. She knew it was late—very late. And she knew it would be morning soon. It didn't take the watch to remind her of that.

If only he weren't next door. If only she didn't have to think about him being on the other side of that wall, lying on his bed, his shirt off, his body warm from sleep. . . . But maybe he, too, was lying awake, thinking of her, building the same erotic images of them in his own mind.

Though she had opted to make a sandwich here for dinner, she knew he had gone out for the evening and had taken Abeline with him. She also knew that it had been very late when they returned, and that, after he put his daughter to bed, he had stood out by the stall talking to Bittersweet. By the animated discussion he was having with the horse, she suspected he was drunk. Had he gone to Eddie's? Had he danced with one of those women Abe insisted were always after him?

She flipped over onto her stomach, bunching up the pillow as the thoughts churned through her mind. She kept trying to fit all the pieces of that man together. What she had seen of him here was not the image Abe had painted of him. He had been a veterinarian, living in a big white house in a large town, married to a pretty wife . . . who had left him for another man. Why? Had he cheated on her? Was she paying him back? Would they reconcile their differences and get back together again? Maybe that was what he was waiting for. Maybe he lived for the day when he and his wife would be together again, the three of them a family once more. Maybe that was why this afternoon he had told her he didn't want or need her in his life right now.

She closed her eyes, remembering every touch of his hands, the urgent stroke of his fingertips, the hunger of his mouth on hers. Was she only serving as a substitute? A surrogate wife and lover? She had known him for only a few short days and had kissed him only twice. She did not want to get involved with him. And yet she was aware of a possessiveness that was totally unfamiliar to her. She didn't want to think of him eating dinner tonight with another woman. She didn't want to think of his arm around another shoulder. She especially did not want to think of him lying in a big firm bed in a clean white house, holding his wife's body next to him.

A shiver of desire ran through her as her body cried out for his touch. If only he could afford to buy her half of Bittersweet. Then she could be gone. She could take the money, resume her life in New York, and forget all about him. Forget this past week ever happened. Forget the touch of his hands and his mouth and . . .

The need to forget carried her into a fitful sleep, full of dream fragments. There was a shelf lined with photographs. There was her father with the President of the United States. There was a little girl with red hair at a birthday party, one of the parties her father had been unable to attend because he was working. There was another picture of a little girl in overalls, standing next to a man with dark brown eyes. Alison was standing on the other side of the girl, but she was falling, her part of the photograph having been viciously hacked off with a pair of scissors. She was falling, falling into a red pit, deeper and deeper while Jake and Abe and William stood at the rim watching her tumble. She woke with a start when she heard the gentle tapping at her door. She sat up and noticed the light edging its way around the flowered curtain, a single shaft of white angling across the red countertop.

"Yes?"

"Ali? It's me. Abeline Koske."

Alison shook the disturbing dream from her mind and smiled to herself. "Come on in, Abeline."

The door opened a crack and a pair of eyes peeked through before opening it farther. Abe, dressed in a pair of purple pants and a lighter purple blouse, stepped into the room.

"Don't you look pretty," Alison said sleepily. "I like your hair that way."

Abe shifted nervously and searched in vain for some pockets to cram her fists into. "I can't do it as good as you. The barrette keeps falling out."

"Come over here and let me see if I can fix it."

Abe walked to the bed and sat down, and Alison sat up behind her, stretching. She pulled more hair into the barrette's clasp. "There you go." She yawned. "How come you're up so early?"

"It's not early. It's after eight o'clock."

"Really?" Alison reached for her watch on the counter. It seemed as if she had just fallen asleep.

"I've been up forever." Abe frowned. "Dad won't get up. He doesn't feel so hot this morning. Told me I was making too much racket. Hey, I've got a great idea! Me and you could go get some breakfast and bring some back to him. We could take the truck. He won't care."

Alison yawned and stretched again, realizing she didn't feel so hot this morning either, even though she hadn't had anything to drink. But Abe was bored. She had no one to play with, no one to talk to. Her father was lying in bed with a hangover and all she wanted to do was go get some breakfast. Alison would feel like a real heel if she said no. Besides that, she could go for a nice hot breakfast herself right now. Since she'd come here her dietary habits had not been the best, and they could use a little improvement.

"Okay," she agreed, slowly tossing the cover back. "Just give me a few minutes to get ready and I'll meet you at the truck." A stable tack room was not the most desirable of living quarters. The biggest disadvantage in Alison's mind was that the bathroom was in another building. That meant grabbing up all of her clothes and toiletries and a towel and trekking in a bathrobe halfway across the fairgrounds. A month ago she would have been appalled if anyone had told her she would be living like this. Come to think of it, she was still appalled. But she was doing it.

Disgusted, Alison looked down at the lump on the bed. "You must have really tied one on last night." She picked up the empty bottles and piles of trash and threw them away. Abe set the styrofoam container of food beside him and went to the refrigerator to pour him a glass of orange juice.

"Yeah, what of it?" Jake grumbled, sitting up with covers pulled up to his waist.

She tried not to look at his bare chest, tried not to think about how warm it would feel against the palm of her hand. His hair was tousled and his cheeks and chin were shadowed with the night's growth of beard. "Nothing," she said, trying hard to sound indifferent. "Just a passing observation. It makes no difference to me what you do. If you want to drink yourself to death, it's your business."

He glared up at her as if she were some sort of puritanical temperance crusader. "You're damn right it's my business. Now," he growled, opening the box of food, "what'd you bring me to eat?"

"Are you always so disagreeable in the morning or do I bring out the worst in you?"

Abe handed him his juice and looked up at Alison. "He used to be the first one up at home, right, Dad?"

His monosyllabic mutter could have been either a yes or a no.

Alison made a wry face. "Must just be me, then."

The forkful of eggs was held suspended between styrofoam plate and mouth as he looked up at her, his eyes dark and full of an emotion she couldn't read. She felt the blood drain from her face and then rush back in, her body running from hot to cold to hot again. She couldn't decipher what was in his dark brown stare, but she had to look away. She could not stand the intensity.

She grabbed a broom and starting sweeping the dirt into big piles.

"And just what do you think you're doing?" he demanded.

"I'm trying to clean up this pigsty you live in, that's what."

"I happen to like this pigsty, if you don't mind. And it's a hell of a lot better than living in that— that—bordello of yours next door."

"Bordello!" she cried indignantly.

"Yeah, plug in a red light bulb and you'd be in business."

Alison began to sputter in rage, but Abe defused the volatile situation with her insatiable curiosity. "What's a bordello?"

Jake glanced at his daughter. "A cathouse." He chuckled to himself. "Alison's new home away from home."

"What's a cathouse?" Abe asked, looking up at Alison's tight mouth. But Jake answered.

"A place where ladies entertain men," Jake said, taking another bite of eggs.

Alison shoved the broom back into its corner of the room. "A place I'm sure your father knows intimately," she countered.

"Oh," Abe said, nodding her head, finally understanding. "A flophouse. Well, why didn't you say so?"

Jake's fork stopped in midair, and he and Alison stared mutely at the girl as she walked over to her bed and started picking up the dirty clothes on the floor around it.

Jake cleared his throat and tried to concentrate on his food. "Right," he mumbled.

"Well," Alison began, then fell silent as she forgot what she was going to say. She tried again. "Guess I'll, uh, go get Bittersweet out and ready to go."

"I've already cleaned her stall, Ali," Abe said. "We don't train her on weekends. She likes to rest."

"Oh," she said, suddenly wondering how on earth she was going to occupy herself for a whole weekend without some project. What did one do in a vacuum of a town like Bartholomew?

Jake was busy eating and Abe was now sitting on her cot, swinging her legs back and forth, chattering away. "Dad and me always go to the farm to camp on weekends, right, Dad?"

Another unintelligible reply came from his throat.

"I didn't know you had a farm," Alison said,

speaking to Abe since Jake seemed to have forgotten how to speak English.

"It's the one we're gonna buy," she explained. "Dad and me are gonna start a breeding farm someday. We're gonna have lots of horses. It's real neat out there."

"I'm sure it is," Alison murmured, feeling a sense of panic rising in her. What was she going to do here all alone this weekend? Alone with a stableful of horses. Maybe she could go up to Chicago. That was it. She could go shopping, go to dinner. Of course, she hated to use her money for the plane ticket, but . . . maybe she could drive. "What did you say?" she asked, realizing that Abe had said something to her.

"I said you ought to go with us. Ya know?"

"Go with you where?"

A heavy sigh fell from her mouth. "To the farm, Ali. Haven't you heard a word I've been saying?"

"Oh—yes, of course I have. But . . ."

"She could go, couldn't she, Dad? You'd love it out there, Ali. It's so much fun."

She was flustered by the invitation and her eyes automatically skipped over to Jake.

"I had thought I'd go, uh, shopping."

"Shopping!" he cried. "Here?"

"Well, I was thinking about driving up to Chicago."

"In what? That cheap heap you rented?"

"Yes."

He chuckled. "Good luck." He ran his gaze down the front of her. "What do you want new clothes for, anyway? You aiming for Bartholo-

107

mew's best-dressed list? I might as well tell you, you've already made that . . . along with a few other lists," he mumbled.

"What kind of lists?" she asked suspiciously.

"You've made quite an impression here. Everybody's talking about you . . . especially since you moved in out here."

"What are they saying?"

He stood up and stretched, then glanced at Abe. "Well, for one thing, they're saying we've got something going between us."

"That's absurd!"

He stared at her for a long moment, his eyes trailing down her body as if he were mentally stripping her and raking her flesh with his dark eyes. "Yeah," he finally said. "That's exactly what I told them." He shrugged. "Anyway, you're welcome to go camping with us if you want. Or go shopping . . . it's no big deal."

Abe had jumped off her cot and was pleading with her. "Please, Ali. You don't want to go to Chicago by yourself, do you?"

"Well . . ." Alison hedged, not wanting to disappoint Abe, and at the same time not wanting to give Jake the satisfaction of making some snide remark about her thinking she was too good for camping. But how could she spend a night camping with him? How could she put them both in that position? Of course, it was ridiculous to try to avoid him. It would be impossible. They had to work the horse together, for heaven's sake. They lived next door to each other, with only a wall separating their private lives. She might as well

108

get used to being around him on a strictly platonic level. They would just have to learn to be together as business partners . . . nothing more.

She hesitated a few seconds longer while he pretended not to be waiting for her answer. "Well," she said, "I guess so. If you're sure."

His gaze dropped back to his plate and he shrugged. "Whatever." He tossed the empty styrofoam box into the trash can and stood up, stepping carefully around Alison so as not to touch her. "Let's get packing," he said, and grabbed a six-pack of beer from the refrigerator and carried it straight out to the truck.

"That's your idea of packing?" she hollered after him.

He tossed the beer into the front seat of the truck and turned around. "What are you, some sort of Carrie Nation?"

"Living in a bordello? Hardly," she countered sarcastically.

"Hmm, well, maybe you were expecting Dom Pérignon."

"Oh," she responded snidely. "You've heard of it."

"I've heard of it," he said, tossing a couple of sleeping bags into the back of the truck. "I just can't afford it." He chuckled at a new thought. "And neither can you."

"Not right now," she conceded. "But I will as soon as we sell Bittersweet."

"Maybe nobody will want to buy her." He grinned at the thought. "Then, instead of sipping your Rothschild and Moët and Chandon, you'll be

109

sucking Mogen David with me." He laughed again. "Yep, that would be a sight to see."

Alison wasn't laughing. The thought was not only intolerable, it was terrifying.

She stood aside, ineffective around Abe and Jake, who were running back and forth from the tack room and the storeroom, gathering up picnic supplies and fishing equipment, acting like a couple of school kids who were finally let out for recess. Abe had a grin from ear to ear and Jake was now whistling, "I Dream of Jeanie with the Light Brown Hair," and he and Abe joked with each other in a way that made them seem more like best friends than father and daughter.

"Here, Your Highness, join in." Jake tossed a third sleeping bag out the door to Alison. "Nobody rides in my truck for free."

She tried to stay detached from the fun of it all, tried not to be affected by his carefree attitude. But when he smiled at her like that, her insides almost flipped over. He was so handsome, so roughly masculine, and there was more than a hint of wild country youth still riding high and fast inside him.

They left the fairgrounds around ten and stopped in town because Jake insisted he wasn't taking Alison anywhere until she got herself a decent pair of shoes—meaning tennis shoes. "You can wear your Pierre Cardin separates, but you are not going to walk around on my land in those ballet slippers or whatever you call them."

"Shoes."

"Really?" he mocked. "You could've fooled me."

110

Once they were in the truck again and driving down the highway, Jake coerced them into singing "Ninety-nine Bottles of Beer on the Wall" with him. When Alison was too hoarse to continue, Jake and Abe sang along with the country songs on the radio, while she watched the passing scenery through the window. She had never felt this kind of laid-back contentment. It wasn't like the things she did at home. This was less exciting to be sure, but it was also less demanding. No one expected her to be witty or wild. In fact, no one expected her to say or be anything. For the first time she could remember in her life, she was free to be alone with her own thoughts.

She had always been an outgoing person, striving hard at a young age to replace the attention she didn't get at home. So she became the life of the party, wild and crazy and abandoned, assuring a place for herself in a world that expected and demanded something from everyone. She would have drowned in the sea of mediocrity had she not found her own special role. She became Alison McKinsey, outrageously extravagant with her money, eager to take off at a moment's notice, always ready to go and do and indulge. She couldn't even remember the last time she had stopped to reflect on where she was going or where she had been. Maybe never. She had been on a roller coaster, always sliding down the steepest track at breakneck speed, screaming with delight at the tumult it created inside her and all around her, and scared to death of what might happen when the ride stopped.

111

Here there were no hills, no joyrides, no screaming drops and jolts against which to constantly brace oneself. Here it was flat, even, steady, unassuming, and quiet. Until today, she hadn't realized how badly she needed to get off the roller coaster for a while. Just to rest.

"This is where I grew up," Jake said as they drove through a wide spot in the road. "Don't blink now. You might miss it."

"Look, Dad, there's your school."

Alison followed the direction of Abe's finger. "That's where you went to grade school?" she asked.

"Yep. A long, long time ago," he murmured, quietly reflecting on the memories this passage inspired.

"My Dad's forty years old," Abe explained, unaware of the grimace on Jake's face.

"Yep," he sighed. "It's all downhill from here on. See that creek over there? We used to dig for worms and drop them down the girls' dresses."

Alison laughed. "You must have been very popular."

"Only with the fast girls." He grinned wickedly.

"You don't say."

"Yeah, we seemed to have found a—a mutual interest."

"Oh." She smiled back. "And what was that?"

"He kissed 'em all!" Abe squealed, bending over with laughter.

"Only a few of them," he countered, turning the corner onto Main Street. "Wow! This place gets smaller every time I come back here. I swear it's shrinking. Look at that building over there. When I was a kid, that was at least four stories tall. Now it's just a squatty two-story."

"Oh, Dad." Abe grinned, elbowing him in the side. "You say that every time we come through here. I don't believe you."

Alison was watching him, wondering what his childhood must have been like. How different it would have been growing up in a place like this. "Was it fun?"

"What's that?" he asked, glancing over at her.

"Growing up here. Were you happy?"

He shrugged. "Sure. You know, the all-American type of life. Uneventful. But yeah, happy. How about you?"

She turned away, looking out the side window. "Sure."

There was a light hesitation before he spoke again. "Abe told me your mother died when you were a baby."

"Yes."

"Your father raised you by himself?"

"He and various housekeepers. He was working most of the time."

"You ought to see the picture of her mom," Abe inserted. "Can he see it, Ali?"

"All right." She fished the photograph from her purse and handed it to Abe, who held it up so her father could see.

"Isn't she pretty, Dad?"

"Beautiful." He glanced quickly at Alison. "You must look like your father."

"Unfortunately, yes."

113

Jake frowned. "Why unfortunately?"

Alison shrugged. "I don't know. I've just been reminded all my life of how different I am from my mother. She was very beautiful and elegant and—"

"So are you."

Her gaze jumped to his face in a quick evaluation of his sincerity. "Not in the same way," she murmured. "She was soft, feminine . . . made people want to take care of her . . . or so I've been told."

"That's what you want?" he asked, still frowning at her. "You want to be taken care of?"

She sighed wearily. "Oh, I don't know. Women in this day and age aren't supposed to want that, are they? My father was always bragging to everyone that I was tough, like him." She turned away again and gazed out over the undulating sea of farmland, and her voice became whisper soft. "I think he was wrong."

Abe sensed that something was bothering Alison, although she didn't really understand. "I think you're tough, Ali," she said, adoration pouring from her assurance, like rain on a summer's afternoon.

Alison smiled a thanks down at her, but wished she had never let the conversation move away from the subject of Jake Koske. She did not want to lay herself open for inspection. "Where did you go to college?" she asked, hoping to get him talking again.

"University of Illinois at Urbana."

"Vet school there too?"

"Yep. The whole nine yards."

"Did you mostly doctor dogs and cats or what?"

"I had an office in town . . . in Quincy. And there, I handled domestic animals. But I also traveled to the outlying farms quite a bit. Worked with horses and sheep and pigs . . . you name it."

"Why did you stop working?"

The silence in the cab of the truck was almost deafening. Abe was suddenly staring straight ahead at the radio dial, and Jake's fingers tightened around the steering wheel.

In an attempt to get away from any speculation about her life, she had stepped too far into his. "What I meant was—"

Jake's voice, low and dry, cut through her weaker one. "I stopped working because there no longer seemed any point." There was no anger in his voice. Nothing but a kind of regret over the way his life had gone. "When I turned thirty-nine, there suddenly didn't seem to be much point in anything anymore."

Abe was still staring straight ahead, her doll propped up in her lap, and Alison frantically tried to think of a way to change the subject.

"I like those flowers," she said, pointing to the line of orange blooms bordering the road. "What are they?"

"Daylilies," Jake answered, a wave of relief washing through his voice. "The blooms only last one day and then new ones open the next morning. They grow like weeds around here. The county plows them down about every six weeks, but they keep on coming back up."

115

"No wonder I like them," she murmured, unaware that he was looking over at her, surprised.

"Why is that?"

She was startled when she realized she had spoken aloud. "I don't know," she hedged. "I guess because they're wild and nothing keeps them down."

"Like you?" he ventured.

She looked over at him. His elbow was resting in the open window, his other arm draped casually over the steering wheel, and the wind rustled through his hair. He always looked so relaxed, as if nothing in the world could make him hurry any faster than he wanted to. He lived for the present and saw no reason to rush it through. Only his hands on her body had seemed hurried and frantic, as if the moment would slip through his fingers unless he grasped it tightly and held on for dear life.

The way he was looking at her now was slow and warm and genuinely interested.

"I don't know," she admitted slowly. "I guess in a way."

"Wild and free," he concluded, watching her over Abe's head. "And now you feel that the world is trying to cut you down."

"Not the world," she answered defensively.

"Then who?"

She turned her eyes toward the side window and stared out over the endless fields of new alfalfa and hay. "I don't know. But . . . something."

"You feel trapped here, don't you?"

She swung her eyes toward him and glanced

116

quickly at the young girl between them. Abe was looking up at her, as interested in the answer to that question as her father was.

"That's not fair," Alison said.

"Why?" he asked. "Because I'm asking it in front of Abe? Is it because you're afraid to be truthful with her . . . with us?"

She shook her head and looked straight ahead, grumbling. "I'm not afraid to be truthful. It's just that I don't know how I feel about being here. I don't belong."

"You choose not to belong."

The breeze from the window felt good on her face. It helped clear away the discomforting heat his questions were causing. Why did he start picking and probing and interrogating, especially in front of Abe? She liked the girl. She didn't want to do or say anything to hurt her more than she had already been hurt. And she knew that she was the object of Abe's worship at this point. Still, she couldn't lie. Something about that child—and her father, for that matter—forced honesty from her even when she didn't want to face it. She glanced back at both of them. "Maybe," she answered. "Maybe I don't want to belong here."

Abe punched a button to change the radio station and turned up the volume. The music filled the truck, filling up spaces left gaping among the three of them. It was a long time before any of them spoke again.

After a while they pulled off the main highway and drove for several minutes down a narrow, dusty country road. Alison rolled up her window to keep the dirt from clogging her nose and eyes and throat, but it only swept over the truck and billowed in Jake's open window. Abe began to fidget and squirm the closer they got to their destination. Whatever anxiety she had been feeling earlier was gone now as excitement consumed her.

"See that water tower?" she said, pointing it out for Alison. "That's on the south line of the property. See that row of trees over there? That runs smack through the middle. There's a creek there. See that roof way over there? That's . . ."

Jake finally had to slow her down. "Hold on, Abe. Alison's going to be sick of the place before she even sees it. Here we go." He pulled the truck onto another short dirt road and stopped at the gate. After jumping out of the truck, he unhooked the gate latch and pulled it open. Abe scooted over into the driver's seat, shifted the truck into drive, and pulled it on through, stopping just on the other side of the fence. Jake closed the gate and jumped in behind the wheel. "Pretty good little driver, isn't she?"

"I can't believe it," Alison marveled. "How old did she say she was?"

"She's really thirty." Jake laughed. "She just pretends she's ten so everybody will fawn all over her all the time."

"Ah, Dad." Abe grinned, elbowing him in the side.

"So this is your land?" Alison asked, gazing out over an expanse of brown weeds.

"Not ours yet. But we hope it will be soon."

"Really." Alison cleared her throat and tried to

118

think of something positive to say. "Does the owner care if we're here?"

"Nah. He lets us use the property any time we want. Nobody lives out here anymore. So we can come out and pretend that we own it. Right?" he said, smiling conspiratorially at Abe.

"Right." She glanced up at Alison. "We like to figure out what we're gonna fix up first."

"Oh," Alison said, working hard at diplomacy. "So you are going to—to fix this up."

Jake glanced over and grinned at her expression, then swept his eyes over the land, trying to see it from her perspective. But what he saw was what he had always seen—plentiful pastureland that rose out of a dark green wooded thicket, cut in half by a slow brown creek that wound crookedly in and out of the patches of sunlight. It was a stretch of green and brown that gradually rose to meet the pale blue of the sky, a play of shadow and light, a quiet, pretty spot that was laced with bluegrass and wild chicory, blackberries and daylilies. It was a place he could respect. A place he could call home.

"This is it" was what he finally said, smiling with pleasure at all he saw.

Alison was watching him as he surveyed the property. There was a glow in his brown eyes that she hadn't seen before, and it intrigued her. What was it about this place that was so special? What did he see that she couldn't? They drove over a bridge that spanned a narrow, dirty creek, passed through a grove of withered pine, and climbed a slight rise into a bigger stretch of grass and weeds.

119

At the end of the road sat a two-story house. At one time it had been white, but most of the paint had been stripped away by years of neglect. A porch looped the structure, but sections of it had fallen away from the house. A concrete well sat to the side, and there were several small, dilapidated outbuildings in a semicircle behind the house.

Alison took a deep breath, trying to still the sense of panic that was starting to rise. She wasn't at all sure she wanted to know Jake Koske this well. This place was a glimpse into his hopes and dreams and brought her closer to the edge of some kind of emotional commitment, farther away from all she had known and thought she would always want. Oh, God, what was she doing here!

The moment the truck stopped in front of the house, Jake and Abe bounded out, like a couple of puppy dogs set free. Abe immediately ran off behind the house while Jake unloaded the gear from the back and popped the top on a can of beer. He handed it to Alison and opened another for himself. Alison stood beside the truck and took a deep sip of beer, failing to comprehend what all the excitement was over this place. Was she missing something obvious?

Jake dropped the gear on the ground and came around to stand in front of her. "So what do you think?" He grinned, sweeping his hand about the place. "Isn't it great?"

She nodded, not sure for a minute that she was going to find her voice. "Oh—yes," she finally managed. "It's—it's very . . ."

He looked down at her, regarding her closely.

"Well, I guess it has to grow on you. Come on, I'll show you around."

She reluctantly let him take her arm and lead her toward the house. "Is it safe? I mean—to go inside."

He laughed as if she had made a joke and took a long swig on the beer. He didn't bother to answer her question.

"So this is where you want to have a breeding farm someday?"

"Yep. Right here. It's perfect. Plenty of space, good grasses. The creek's down a bit, but it'll come back with some rain. And I'd put in a pond."

Alison stepped carefully up onto the creaking porch. "I guess you'd tear this down and build a new house."

"Heavens, no," he said, looking shocked that she would even consider such an idea. "I'd fix this one up. It's got lots of character."

"It sure does," she murmured as the screen door fell loose into her hand. "Straight out of *The Grapes of Wrath.*"

Jake just laughed and caught the screen, setting it to the side of the porch before opening the door and leading her inside. "Now, this is the parlor," he said. "But since I don't have much use for one of those, I'd knock this wall out and make these two rooms into one. See?"

Carrying her can of beer, Alison followed him across the oaken floor, still solid though in bad need of varnish. "This would be one big living room then."

"Yeah. And over here is another room. I don't

121

know what I'd do with it. I guess it was a bedroom at one time or another."

"A rather small one," Alison commented dryly. It was about the same size as the walk-in closet in her bedroom at home.

"Yeah, well, Abe will probably claim it for something. Back here is the kitchen." Jake laughed at Alison's horrified expression. "Needs a little updating, doesn't it?"

"Has anyone lived here since the twenties?" she asked, marveling at the antiquated stove and porcelain sink and countertop. "I think I've only seen one of these things in the old movies they show on late-night television."

"I guess you're right." He shrugged. "This is where I'd have trouble fixing it up right. I mean, to me a stove is a stove. I'm not really up on the latest gourmet kitchen designs. Come on, you want to go upstairs?"

"I—suppose," she answered, reluctantly following him. "Goodness, Jake, do you have any idea what it will cost to make this place livable?"

"I know it won't be cheap."

"It would probably be cheaper to tear it down and put up a brand-new one."

"I'm sure you're right, but it wouldn't be half as much fun. This place is a challenge and . . . well, by then maybe I'll be ready for a challenge."

Alison stopped halfway up the stairway and studied his broad back as he climbed toward the second floor. "How long have you been living in a tack room, Jake?"

122

He stopped and turned around. "About a year. Why?"

"That's what I was going to ask you. Why? Why have you been living there?"

"Couldn't afford anyplace else. What little we have in the bank, we're saving to buy this place."

"Couldn't you have—well—worked, continued with your veterinary practice?"

"I will soon. I just needed a rest. Anyway, I lost my practice."

She watched his face and listened to his voice, but he gave no hint of what had happened or what he was feeling. It was as if someone else was saying the words, as if the voice and the person were two separate beings, neither connected in any way to the other.

"How?" she asked, not realizing that she had stepped across the line of polite interest into the realm of needing to know.

He ran his hand along the railing, absorbing the grain of the wood into his palm, and his voice was kept level and dry. "I approached forty and I just let my life fall apart."

"A midlife crisis, you mean?"

He chuckled humorlessly. "They call it a crisis, but I don't know. *Crisis* has such a cataclysmic ring to it. With me, it was kind of a quiet fizzle. I think I just got tired. When my marriage broke up, I started drinking and lost interest in almost everything." He slapped the railing with his hand. "Well, shall we forge ahead with the tour?"

She watched him turn and climb the last three

stairs. "If it makes you feel any better," she called after him, "my life isn't so hot right now either."

He reached the top and stopped, but didn't look back. "Why would that make me feel better?"

"I don't know," she said, climbing after him. "Misery loves company, and all that."

He finally turned as she reached the top of the steps. He was less than a foot away from her and she had to tilt her head back to look up at him. "Are you miserable?" he asked, his eyes darkly serious.

"I don't know," she said. "I never thought I was. There—there wasn't time for that."

"Too busy having fun?"

She smiled thinly. "Yes."

"Maybe that's the way to do it, then. Fill your hours with so much fun that you don't have time to be unhappy."

"Yes," she said. "As long as you don't ever stop running. If you do, it'll catch up with you."

He took a deep breath and let it out slowly. Gazing across the landing to the room beyond, he said softly, "God, I love this place. Someday . . . someday it's going to be mine." He looked back at her and grinned. "After we make our fortune with Bittersweet."

"Are we going to make a fortune, Jake?"

"I doubt it. But it's a start, at least." He led the way into the first bedroom, a small room with a large window and peeling wallpaper. "Is a fortune all that important to you?"

"I've always had money. Lots of it."

"What happened to it?"

She stood in front of the window and crossed her arms as she looked down at the side yard. "My attorney says I squandered it away. 'Frivoled' is what he called it."

"Did you?"

"Half of it."

"And the other half?"

She sighed heavily and moved away from the window. "I have to show I can make something on my own before I get the rest of my inheritance. Make something out of nothing, the way my father did, William said."

"Who's William?"

"My attorney."

"Ah. So, once you make some money with Bittersweet, you're home free. You'll get the rest of your inheritance."

She glanced at him, but his face was as expressionless as the gray field that lay to the west of them. Home, yes. But free? She wasn't sure. She nodded anyway. "Yes."

He turned to the window and rested his hands on the sill as he peered down at the yard below. Looking past him, Alison could see Abe running around the well, her hand touching every third brick as she circled it.

"You know," he said, "I never even knew her until about a year ago."

Alison frowned behind him. "Who?"

"Abe."

"I don't understand. I thought you were her—"

"Father?" he finished for her. "Yeah, I was. But in name only. I was so wrapped up in my own life.

I had my vet practice. I went to the track in the evenings and on weekends to help out with some of the horses. There was an old guy there—Teddy Rawlings—and he taught me everything I know about training."

"So you didn't see much of your daughter?"

He shook his head. "No. Her mother was the real parent. I was just the one who came around for a meal now and then." He paused for a moment. "And the one she could probably hear arguing with her mother late at night." He hung his head between his arms and dropped his gaze to the floor. "Then all of a sudden, I was all she had, and she was all I had."

Alison's hand lifted easily and naturally to his back. "She adores you."

"I can't imagine why," he said in a self-deprecating tone. "I'm not much of a father."

"I guess children can put up with just about anything if they know they are loved."

He turned around to face Alison. "I do love her."

"She knows that, Jake."

His eyes narrowed on her face and his head was cocked to the side. "You told me I was a worthless excuse for a father."

"I was angry." She shifted nervously and clenched her hands in front of her. "I—I've always gotten my way and—well, when I don't, I get mad. I sometimes say things that—"

"You were right," he said. "I have been a worthless excuse for a father. That kid deserves better."

126

"If it makes any difference, Jake, I've reevaluated my opinion. I think you're a terrific father."

"What changed your mind?"

"Just watching you with her. You're so honest with each other. You're good friends and you have a rapport between you that . . . well, I think I'm a little envious. I never had that with my father, or with anyone."

He regarded her for a long moment, piecing together the puzzle of her in his mind. After a moment, the pieces became jumbled, mingling with the more basic urges she stirred up in him.

His eyes darkened and she became aware of the exaggerated rise and fall of his chest. She started to turn away, but the husky timbre of his voice captured her, holding her imprisoned before him.

"What do you think of the bedroom?"

Her own breath accelerated and a live coal was carried through her bloodstream. "I—it's . . ."

He stepped closer and his hands slid slowly up her arms to her neck. "I wish to God there was a bed in here right now," he whispered.

She shook her head, trying to deny the feelings she had, trying to deny that she wanted the same thing.

"Yes, you do," he said, one hand moving around her back and pulling her up close, the other resting against her neck.

She shook her head again. "You were going to try not to—to do this. Remember? You were—" But his mouth came down hard, capturing hers before she could finish. The urgency was back. He was no longer the slow-moving, easygoing Jake

127

Koske. He was a man with a mission, with a driving need that overpowered her senses. His mouth sought her lips again, consuming her with his hunger. "I don't need you," he groaned low and breathlessly in her ear, trying to prove with words what his actions denied. "I don't want to want you. I thought I could stay away. I thought I could keep from touching you. . . ."

The fire from the tips of his fingers spread through her, but she tried to find the breath and the resolve to stop this before they were both sorry. She pushed against him, trying to angle away and out of his arms.

His hands continued to hold her arms as he stared at her, searching desperately for a reason to this obsession, this physical craving he had for her. He didn't need any woman in his life right now. He had already made a mess of one relationship. He didn't want to take the chance of repeating his mistakes. And especially not with this woman. Before long she would be gone, back to the carousel ride that was her life. He didn't need that. He didn't need her. He repeated this over and over to himself, while his body burned with a need of its own.

He pulled her up against him, tightly, one hand moving to the back of her head to hold her still. His mouth swooped down over hers again, capturing it, making it his. And Alison thought she would melt from the feel of him next to her. His fingers dove into her hair and his other hand dropped to cradle her hip, pulling her closer. She wanted to sink into his body, to meld her fire with his.

But she couldn't do this. She had to force herself to be the stronger of the two. He was all wrong for her. And this was the worst form of insanity imaginable.

Alison pulled back and this time managed to edge out of his arms. He tried to reel her back in, but she quickly moved to the far side of the room and ran her hands along the peeling flowered wallpaper, trying to bring her pulse under control, trying to find her breath. Her back was facing him as she spoke. "This is insane, Jake. It's—it's crazy! We've got to stop it right now. You don't want me. I don't want you. It's purely physical." She paused for only a second while she tried to convince herself that it was so. "It cannot go on."

From behind her, she heard his boots tapping across the floor, going through the doorway and descending the stairs. She followed each sound in her mind, concentrating on it, letting it fill her. There was the squeak of the front door and then the tap of boots striding across the porch and down into the dirt yard. And then there were the muffled voices of Abe and Jake as they walked to the truck to pull out the rest of the camping supplies.

Alison couldn't move. Her body still stung from the grip of his fingers; her lips still burned from the fiery hunger of his mouth. She meant what she had said. She didn't want him . . . at least not in her mind. But her mind and her body were telling her totally different things. What her body craved, her mind recoiled from in horror. And what her rational brain told her was the right course of action, her body denied with a thousand pulsating urges.

She didn't want to get involved with a man like Jake Koske. Other than the horse they both owned together, she had nothing in common with him. They were not alike. Their lives were on completely different tracks and always would be. He would never fit into hers, nor she into his. So why was she torturing herself with this senseless longing that would bring nothing but hurt to both of them?

Because—her body screamed—because he is a man unlike any you have ever known. Because when he touches you, he makes you feel alive in a way you never have before. Because being around him makes you look at life in a totally different way, see things you never would have seen otherwise.

She stared out the window at the colorless land he loved so much. In the periphery of her eye she caught sight of something. A splash of bright orange under the noonday sun. A cluster of daylilies straining up through the tall grasses, their orange heads adding color and life to this otherwise gray blotch of weeds. Her heart leapt at the sight of them, and it frightened her. She knew, as she turned away from the window, that she had to leave this place. She had to go back home to the glaring brilliance of her world. It was safer. There her heart did not leap at so simple a sight as a clump of flowers. There she could retreat from these irrational impulses and emotions. She had to go home. Before it was too late.

But she couldn't. Damn it, she couldn't. She could not leave until they sold Bittersweet. She could not go home empty-handed. So she was trapped here—a prisoner of fate and of physical desires that would not set her free.

CHAPTER NINE

The door swung open and she stepped out onto the porch. The sun spotlighted her for the moment, holding her suspended in the white light for him to absorb. She was standing there in her snug blue jeans, pale blue blouse with the cuffs rolled up, the pair of tennis shoes he had insisted that she buy, and that mass of red hair pulled back and clipped at the sides of her head. She was so different from his wife. MaryAnn had been outgoing and earthy, and everyone fell in love with her the minute they met her. She had always been so right for him, or so he had convinced himself. Alison McKinsey, on the other hand, was the antithesis of what he thought he wanted in a woman. Too sophisticated, too polished, too afraid to get down on a level with the rest of humankind. Yet there was something about her that made his skin come alive and his blood bound through his veins merely at the sight of her. He had never felt that way with MaryAnn. Alison was all wrong for him, but damn, she was an intriguing woman!

"How come I have to do all the work?" Abe

complained, climbing back onto the tailgate of the truck to reach for the box of cooking utensils.

"Sorry," Jake mumbled, tearing his eyes away from Alison and back to the task at hand. He took the box from his daughter and set it on the ground under a big oak. When he looked back up, Alison had left the porch and was walking across the yard toward the barn. He watched as she stopped, stooping down to pick a clump of daylilies, tearing off parts of the long stalks to make a manageable bouquet. His body heated up in response to the sight. He wanted to make love to her in every way possible. He wanted to lose himself inside her. He wanted to drag her down into that field of daylilies and explore every part of her among the brilliant orange flowers and swaying grasses. God, he wanted her! He didn't know when in his life he had wanted a woman as badly.

But she was right. They had to cease this madness between them. It would come to no good. They were both adults, and they could control whatever impulses they had around each other. He had to do it for his own self-preservation.

"What about Alison?"

Jake spun around and stared at his daughter, wondering if she had somehow read his mind. "What?" he asked too loudly and harshly.

She just stared back at him from her spot in the back of the truck. "She doesn't have a fishing pole, Dad. What's she gonna use?"

"Fishing—oh," he said, letting his breath out slowly. "Yeah, well, I'll share with her if she wants,

133

but I—I kind of doubt if she's going to want to do much fishing."

"Why not?"

Jake looked at Abe and leaned his elbow on the truck while he debated how to tell her what had to be said. "Abe, I know you like Alison. And, well, I do too, sort of. But . . ." He took a deep breath and wished desperately that Abe's eyes were not so dark and penetrating, not so much like his own. Sometimes she made him feel like a babbling fool. "You know, eventually she is going to leave. Go back home. You realize that, don't you?"

Abe's face was as impervious as petrified wood. "Sure. I'm not stupid."

His breath left him in a heavy sigh. "I know you're not stupid, Abeline. Sometimes I think you're a heck of a lot smarter than I am. It's just that I know you like her a lot and that you probably wish that—"

Abe dropped the fishing-tackle box back onto the bed of the truck with a loud clang. "I know she's gonna leave," she said, scooting to the tail-gate and jumping down onto the ground. "It's no big deal."

Jake watched in silence as his daughter walked away, heading off down the slope toward the creek. He was acutely aware of a huge weight in the center of his chest. A weight that had been there for so long, he now felt it had become an integral part of his body.

The blanket was spread out on a soft grassy mound several yards up from the creek. Abe had

134

finished eating and was sitting on the bank of the creek with a fishing pole in her hand.

Alison leaned back on her hands and closed her eyes, letting the warm breeze drift around her. The smells of the afternoon were heightened by the blowing air, the fragrance of grass and bark and fish and wild strawberries. Ever since she had spotted the daylilies from the bedroom window, she had become aware of things that had eluded her before—the sweet smell of the farm air, the feel of the sun and wind upon her skin, the sight of golden wheatfields swaying in the afternoon breeze, the texture of the grass beneath her fingers. Though the very idea of living in a place like this was beyond her comprehension, there was still something very peaceful about it, something that lifted her soul and infused it with a breath of fresh air.

Jake dropped to the blanket beside her and handed her a new bunch of daylilies.

"Thank you." She smiled, cradling the bundle in her arms.

"To freedom," he said, lying back on the blanket. "To growing free and wild."

"Is that the way you feel when you're out here?"

"Yeah, I love it. Now if I had a few broodmares, I'd feel even better."

"Sounds like a lot of work."

"It is," he agreed. "But delivering foals is a good kind of work. I don't think I'd ever get tired of that. It was the people who mistreated their pets who really got to me when I had the office in Quincy. People who would buy their kids a dog or cat and then not even bother to take care of it. I lost a lot of clients just because I couldn't keep from telling them off half the time." —

Alison smiled at that. "I'll bet you were a good doctor."

He hesitated before responding. "Yeah, I was. I will be again, too . . . someday." He looked away, closing the subject.

Alison astutely switched topics. "Abe really seems to like it out here."

"Yeah. It's good for her. I want her to have lots of quiet and plenty of space to figure out what she wants out of life. I don't want a lot of social pressure put on her. I don't like what it does to people."

"Like me?"

Jake's gaze jumped to Alison's face. "I didn't say that."

"But it's what you meant. And . . . maybe you're right. I do feel pressure to act and be a certain way. It's a matter of survival."

"Living shouldn't be that hard, Alison."

"I never thought it was. It's just different from the way you were raised, that's all. You know, that's one reason I don't feel I belong here. Everyone here equates different with wrong. I'm different, therefore the way I talk and dress and act is immediately suspect."

"You have a point there. I guess we're kind of narrow-minded." He grinned over at her. "I'll work on that, okay?"

She swallowed hard. No, don't, she wanted to

136

say. Don't work on anything. Don't make me like you any more than I already do.

She watched him lying beside her on the blanket, his forearm now shielding the sun from his eyes. The sun on his hair brought out gold highlights that she hadn't noticed before, and his skin was bronze and roughly textured. His left hand rested lightly on his stomach and she had an urge to replace it with her own. He looked warm and hard and inviting.

"Jake?" she whispered softly, in case he was asleep.

He lifted his arm and peered up at her. Tiny lines fanned out from the corners of each eye as he squinted into the sun.

She wanted to stare at him forever, wanted to drink in the sight of him while she had the chance, but she dropped her gaze to the flowers in her lap and searched for the right words. "I was just wondering. Are you—divorced?"

It was a moment before he answered. "Yes."

She nodded slowly, knowing his answer should not matter to her in the least. But it did. "Did it end—badly?"

"Yes." He shrugged. "But then it had been bad for years, so it couldn't have ended any other way."

"I'm sorry."

He raised himself up on one elbow and regarded her carefully. "Why?"

She frowned at the question, not knowing quite how to answer it. "I guess because I was thinking about Abeline, and about you. It must be hard on everyone when there's a child involved."

He stared toward the creek. They could just see the tip of Abe's head where she sat on the bank, waiting for a fish to latch on to the worm she had dug up from the soft, wet mud. "You know," he said slowly, "MaryAnn just got up one day and left. No note, no good-bye to Abe. Nothing. She just pulled up stakes."

"With a man, Abe said."

He glanced over at Alison, sitting so still, her mouth tight, poised as if the statement had come reluctantly from her. "That's right. With a man. One of a long line of many."

"That's horrible. How could she do that to her own daughter? To you?"

"Me, I can understand. I wasn't the most attentive husband. My vet practice and the horses I helped to train were my life. I guess I just didn't give her what she needed in a man. But Abe— that's the part I'll never understand. She's never even called her or tried to contact her in any way. After the divorce decree became final, I lost track of her. She just breezed off somewhere."

"What was she like as—as a person? How did you meet?"

Jake plucked a long blade of grass and began mechanically chewing on it. He was staring off over the field of wild flowers tucked in between the tall grasses, his eyes narrowed on a vision of the past. "It was a small town. We grew up together. She was a cheerleader, very pretty, one of the popular ones. Everybody loved MaryAnn. It

138

was always—assumed that we would marry. Everyone had made us a couple even before we had a chance to decide if that was what we really wanted." He tossed away the chewed grass and plucked another from the ground. "She wanted me to go into her father's banking business after high school, but I had other plans. I had always wanted to be a veterinarian. I guess that's part of the problem with relationships at that age. You don't really talk. Not about the important things. I had never confided in her, never told her what I wanted out of life." He glanced at Alison, but his fleeting smile was directed at his own folly. "So I went on to college, married her when I was a senior, and then dragged her along while I went to vet school. She hated all of it. It caused a rift that never closed up. It was always there between us, leaving a big hole for all the other problems to fall into. . . ."

Alison concentrated on an ant that was inching its way along a thin blade of grass, and tried not to think about what she was going to suggest, or to feel anything in his response. "Maybe someday she'll come back, sorry for the way things went."

He shrugged. "Maybe."

She swallowed hard, watching the ant curve over the tip and follow the shaft back down to its base. "I suppose you hope that she will. That things will be different this time."

She felt the heat from his stare and her face turned toward him. He was watching her so closely, his eyes dark and questioning. "No, Alison, I don't hope that at all. The marriage was over long before it was legally dissolved. One man didn't satisfy her." He broke the blade of grass between his fingers and threw it away. "Doesn't do much for the ego, I assure you. Nevertheless . . . that's the way it was."

She swung her gaze toward the creek and kept it there, her heart pounding fearfully in her chest. "What about you?" she heard him say.

She looked back at him. "What do you mean?"

He cocked his head. "The man or men in your life . . . anyone special?"

She shook her head and looked down at the flowers. "No. I seem to be able to—to capture men's attention easily, but I don't keep it for very long."

"Why not?"

"I don't know. I'm not like your MaryAnn. People don't automatically love me."

He looked thoughtful. "Maybe you don't want them to. Maybe you're afraid."

She glanced up sharply at him, then looked away toward the creek. "I think . . . the sooner we sell Bittersweet, the—the—"

"The better?"

"Yes."

His eyes were fastened on her profile, probing beneath the set lips and jaw. He wondered what had made her say that. Was it the things he had said about MaryAnn? About himself? The things about her? Why, every time he looked at her, did she appear as if she wanted to bolt and run?

"Abeline is starting to grow attached to me and—"

140

"And you can't handle that, right?" His sharp voice was almost unrecognizable, even to him. Was that really the reason? Did it all have to do with commitment on her part, or was that only an excuse to cover the fact that she didn't like it here?

She looked over at him. His face was held rigid, his eyes dark and glowering. She looked down at her hands clenched in her lap. "I don't know. I've never had anyone, well, need me before. I've always been free and on my own. I think that Abeline has transferred some of her need for a mother onto me." She looked up at him beseechingly. "I don't want to hurt her, Jake."

His words dropped like harsh blows onto her upturned face. "I wouldn't worry about Abe if I were you. She's a survivor. No, Alison, if I were you, I'd think about who it is you're really trying to protect. You're not worried about a ten-year-old girl. You're worried about your own damn hide." He reached for his fishing pole, then strode off briskly toward the creek.

Alison, shocked into utter silence, watched him go. When she was finally able to stand on her less than steady legs, she saw that they were sitting side by side, father and daughter, their backs rigid and unbending against the rest of the world.

He lay in his sleeping bag with his hands locked behind his head, listening to the sounds of sleep coming from the child beside him. On the other side of Abe was Alison, but he purposely tried not to listen at all for any sounds of her breathing. He didn't even want to acknowledge the fact that she was there on the same patch of ground as he.

It would be best for everyone concerned when she finally went back to New York where she belonged. There would be no need for her to stay on once she sold her half of Bittersweet . . . other than the fact that he had gotten used to her . . . other than the fact that, despite what he knew was best for everyone, he wanted her to stay . . . other than the fact that when she left, there would be another hole in his life to plug up, another piece of him gone.

He had tried not to like her, he really had. In fact, in the beginning he hadn't even had to work hard at it. She had grated on his nerves from the moment she forced her way into his life. So when and how had it moved from irritation to attraction? Yes, she was beautiful, but MaryAnn had been beautiful in her own way too. And yes, she was rich, but then wealth—especially the inherited kind—had never impressed him much. What was it about her that continually nagged at him, that kept him awake nights, that inched through his bloodstream like a live wire? She didn't belong here. She needed the big-city lights and a kind of frenetic excitement that he had never known and didn't even care to experience. Despite his own downhill slide of the past year or two—the drinking after MaryAnn had left—he was content with life here. He liked the simple pleasures—catching a fish for dinner, truck rides through the countryside, a warm female body next to him at night, a friendly game of cards at Eddie's, a kid to share the good times with. He didn't need anything more than that. So it shouldn't matter in the least that Alison McKinsey, New York socialite, was eventually going to leave. It shouldn't matter, but it did.

He watched the gray clouds moving across the darker sky, and within minutes a large drop of water hit him in the face. It was followed by others.

"Abe," he called, shaking her by the shoulders. "Hop up, babe. It's starting to rain. We'd better get inside."

He started to touch Alison to wake her, but she sat up before he could reach her. "What is it? Oh, is it raining?"

"Yes, let's get our sleeping bags inside the house." He had already bundled up his own and was reaching for Alison's. "Help Abe with hers."

Alison let him take her sleeping bag, and she bent down to help Abe fold hers up. Together they carried it into the house just before the rain started to fall heavily. They laid out their sleeping bags on the floor of the parlor, wiped themselves off with a big towel, and lay back down, listening to the sounds of the storm raging outside.

Abe fell back asleep within minutes, but with each new clap of thunder Alison bolted upright and hugged her knees with her arms.

"There's no need to be afraid," Jake whispered, propping up on one elbow, watching her face and body come aglow in the bright flashes of lightning. "We're safe in here."

The next flash illuminated her profile. She was

looking up, as if expecting the ceiling to crash in upon them any second now.

"This house has withstood a lot of storms, Alison. Try to get some sleep."

She lay back down on the bedroll, but he could tell she had not gone back to sleep.

After an hour, the storm passed. The clouds rolled away and a velvet, starlit sky was left behind. He watched her as she stood up, pulled the bedroll around her shoulders, and walked out the door onto the porch. He heard the creak of the steps as she stepped down into the rain-soaked yard. And he knew that, even though he would probably regret it in the morning, he was going to get up and follow her.

Alison walked out into the yard. The grass was wet and cool against her bare feet. The air smelled clean and minty, and a whole canopy of stars was spread across the sky above her. The bank of clouds in the west rolled away and left a cool, white moon hanging in the open space. She breathed deeply, letting the air fill her lungs and throat and nose. She hadn't slept at all tonight, and it had nothing to do with the storm. It had to do with Jake Koske. It had to do with the thought of sometime soon saying good-bye to him . . . and to Abeline. When had that man and his daughter become so important in her life? It had not been a conscious effort on her part, that was for sure. She had not wanted to feel anything special for that little girl. And she certainly had not wanted to feel anything but professional courtesy toward Jake

Koske. When had all of that changed and grown to new and unmanageable proportions?

He had redefined all of her ideas of what a man should be. He was not rich. He already had a child. He wore cowboy boots and fished on the bank of a sluggish brown creek. He lived in a tack room and drank tequila to ward off the ghosts of his past. He was big, with hands that took what they wanted. He was everything the other men she had known were not.

It was funny, in a way. Here she was in the heartland of America, where life was supposed to be easier and simpler, and yet her own life had never been more complicated.

She took another deep breath and crossed her arms over her chest. It was crazy, really. Why did she need this man's touch so desperately? She had been with other men and never felt the driving need she had with Jake. Maybe once she got back to New York, it would diminish. Then she could stop anticipating the touch of his hands and mouth on her at every turn.

As if her thoughts had come alive, she felt his large hand on the blanket at her shoulder. She spun around in the slick, wet grass and stared up at him. The moonlight highlighted the angles of his face while his eyes were left in shadow. His feet, too, were bare and he wore only a pair of jeans. She knew if she reached out to touch his chest, it would be cool from the night air.

"Aren't you cold?" he asked gently, his voice filled with a lover's concern.

She let out an uneven breath. "No. The blanket keeps me warm. But you—you must be freezing."

"Not really. I was worried about you out here. Are you all right?"

"Fine."

"Good."

She nodded and looked away, off toward the row of trees that edged the creek. But her eyes were drawn back to his chest, bare and dark. She just wanted to touch it once. Just to see how cold his skin felt. Nothing more. Just one touch.

She reached her hand out from the warm bedroll and laid it flat against his skin, the heat from her palm transmitting into that spot on his chest. She heard his sharp intake of breath and felt the rapid pounding of his heart beneath her hand.

His hands came up to rest on her shoulders, two heavy boulders that held her down when what she really wanted was to fly away as fast as she could to safer heights.

"It would be better if I could leave, Jake. If I could go back to New York. Now."

"Yes."

Her fingers trailed through the matted hair on his chest. "It would be better for all concerned."

His breathing accelerated and one of his hands lowered, slipping around her neck and sliding down the front of her chest. His fingers dipped between the thick folds of the bedroll. "I agree," he murmured huskily.

"I—I'm glad we've never—done anything that we would regret later."

"Me too," he said, his fingers sliding over her

breast, which was covered only by the thin cotton T-shirt he had loaned her.

Her skin immediately drew taut from his touch and her breath clogged in her throat. His hand was there to catch her head when it dropped back. Her eyes closed as he drew lazy, erotic patterns with his fingers across her breasts, moving back and forth from one to the other. The bedroll had slipped unnoticed off her shoulders and lay in a heap on the wet ground at her feet.

"I don't intend to do anything I'll regret, Jake."

"I know," he whispered, lowering his mouth to her arched neck. "Me either."

"We mustn't let . . . we can't . . . let this go too far."

His lips trailed across her throat and onto her shoulder while his fingers slid down her stomach and abdomen and then lower still between her thighs. "No," he breathed against her flesh. "We won't."

Immediately he pulled her against him and his mouth moved roughly over her lips with uncontained urgency. "I just wanted one touch," she moaned against his parted lips. "Nothing more."

A half-muffled groan ripped from his throat. "No more," he murmured against her ear. "Just one touch. No more."

"Yes." She sighed, oblivious now of all but the magic of his fingers as they intimately explored her body, penetrating it completely, making it his.

"Yes," he groaned, lowering her to the ground onto the bundle of bedroll that cushioned their bodies from the wet earth. "Yes," he said, forming the words against her mouth.

The wild fluttering of the owl in the tree above them matched the beat of her heart as she felt the T-shirt lifted from her body. No, she had not wanted this man or his touch. She had wanted to retain her ideas of what a man should be. She did not want this drastic change in her life. And yet, his mouth closing over her breast filled her with a completeness she had never even imagined.

And so she reached for him, blindly, urgently. She helped him take off his jeans and let him pull her back down on the ground with him. She ran her hands along the angles of his body and delighted in the low moans her touch invoked. Don't ever stop holding me! she wanted to cry. Don't ever stop making me feel this way.

"Don't go away," he whispered fervently against her neck. "Don't go home, Alison. Stay."

She wrapped her arms around his neck and held him tightly. And suddenly he was there. With her. Inside her. Filling her. They moved together against the wet yielding ground beneath them. The two of them. This smalltown man who lived in a stable and loved this humble patch of land . . . and this sophisticated woman who thought she needed dazzling lights and never-ending activity . . .

Together, they fused their lives into one.

And the colors burst before her eyes, a brilliant display of dancing lights and dazzling yellows and oranges and blues. The pressure of his mouth and hands and body was fiercely possessive, as if he would never let her go, as if he would hold her here, making her his own forever.

And she realized with a frightening intensity that if he asked her to stay, if he would simply say the words, she would never go. Never. In this moment of blind passion and love, she knew that whatever he asked of her, she would do. And while her body and heart screamed over and over for him to ask her to stay, her unwilling mind prayed fervently that he would release his tight grip on her and let her fly away.

CHAPTER TEN

The long warm days that followed melded into a pattern like the mellow border of a patchwork quilt. Alison would awaken early to the sounds of the roosters crowing outside the stable. She would dress and eat and then work all day beside Jake and Abe, pacing Bittersweet, turning her, timing her, cleaning the stall, washing her down after her workout and then, bone tired at the end of the day, fall asleep only to awaken early the next day to repeat the pattern.

On weekends they would all pile into Jake's truck and drive to the farm, where they would explore the creek, pick wild flowers, fish, and chop firewood, and Alison would listen with increasing fascination to Jake and Abe's plans for the breeding farm they would one day own.

Alison's body fell into the circadian rhythm of country living, her breathing slowed to the pace set by the warm afternoons, her appetite grew in proportion to the work they had done that day, and her mind flowed easily with the current of the rust-colored creek as it wound its way through the willows and river birch.

There was one thing that had not fallen into the pattern, one part of her body and soul that had not been sewn into the tapestry of their days. Since that night on the farm almost a month before, she and Jake had not touched each other in any way other than the most perfunctorily or professional. It had been a mistake. They both knew it, and neither of them had wanted to establish a physical relationship that would tear at the seams when she finally went away. They both insisted that it had been a mistake, and they took great pains to deny what they both still craved. Whenever he was near, she longed to reach out for him and burned with an electric shock if he accidentally brushed against her. While the professional side of their relationship had grown into an easy, friendly form of cooperation, the personal side had taken on dimensions of torturous proportions. It was a physical and emotional pain unlike any she had ever known. She marveled at how in one respect she could feel so relaxed and at ease in his company, and at the same time feel as if a thousand dull-edged knives were being thrust into her body.

On this Thursday afternoon, it was raining. Driving sheets of rain cascaded in a constant flow from the lead-gray sky, and the mud around the stable splattered up with each successive wave that fell. Alison was leaning against the stall gate, watching Jake fit a new shoe to Bittersweet's hoof. The sound of the rain pinging on the tin roof and the rhythmic clang of Jake's hammer striking the horseshoe, provided an insulating warmth that wrapped around her like a wool blanket.

"Horses aren't like people," he was telling her while he checked the level of the foot with a trim gauge. "They can't tell you they are ready and in peak form."

"So then how do you know?"

"You can feel it in your hands when you take one around the track. It comes from experience, I guess. Knowing the feel."

"And Bittersweet?" she asked. "Is she ready?"

He let the horse's foot down and looked over at Alison, a smile creasing his tanned skin. "She is most definitely ready."

Alison could hardly contain her excitement. They had all worked so hard with Bittersweet and had put so much hope and anticipation in her success. Now the time was at hand. The horse was ready to race.

"I just hope you and Abe took care of the forms and got us registered on time," he said, checking the hind feet for balance.

"We did. Everything is ready from that end. I just can't believe it. I can't wait to see her actually run a race."

He smiled at her again. "You've never been to any kind of horse race before?"

"No."

He dropped the leg and leaned against the gate on the opposite side from her. "What kind of things do you do in New York for entertainment?"

"Oh, I go to the theater quite a bit. To restaurants and parties and—"

"You like indoor games, then."

He was regarding her closely and she heard the

shift in his tone. She knew what it signified, knew what he was thinking, wanting, feeling. His voice had a husky quality to it, and his eyes had grown hot and probing.

She knew where this could lead. Her body had been screaming for his touch since that night at the farm and now his hand rested on the top rail of the gate only inches from hers. His face was close and if she leaned toward him, it would be so easy and natural. But it had been wrong before and it would be even more wrong now. They both knew it. So why were they torturing themselves this way?

"After the first race," she began, haltingly and awkwardly. "Uh—will we—offer Bittersweet for—for sale?"

His eyes had been trained on her mouth, but he lifted them to her eyes. "Are you in a hurry to leave?" he asked softly.

She swallowed again. "We've talked about this before, Jake. You know it would be best for—"

"Why?"

She faltered and let out a heavy sigh. "Jake, please . . ."

"I just don't understand, Alison. I'm trying to, really I am, but I just want to know what it is about this place or about me that you find so distasteful."

"That's the wrong word. I don't find this distasteful."

"Then what?"

She lowered her eyes to the floor of the stall and shook her head, whispering. "I don't know. It—it scares me sometimes."

His eyes creased at the edges as he concentrated on her face. "What does? Please tell me, Alison. Are you afraid of me?"

She lifted her eyes to his face and wanted to reach out and lay her hand against his jaw. "It's not you, Jake. It's—well, it's me and the way I feel around you."

His hand moved to cover hers and then slid slowly along her forearm and around the bend of her elbow. Her skin burst into flames at the touch and she wanted to cry out in pleasure-pain. "I know what you feel, Alison. I feel it too. There's nothing wrong with it. It's natural."

She shook her head. "Not for me."

"Why?"

She sighed again. "Oh, Jake, look at me. I don't belong here. This kind of life is not for me."

His fingers closed around her upper arm and he pulled her closer, forcing her to look up at him. Only the gate separated their bodies. "I am looking at you, Alison. That's all I've done for the past month. Now you should take a close look at yourself, at the way you've changed. You were so pale when you first came here. Now you've got a healthy glow to your cheeks. You've developed muscles where I'm sure you never thought you had any before. You're strong and alive and—" His voice broke off and then came back in a low, vibrating whisper. "And so beautiful. You do belong here, Alison, but you've convinced yourself that you don't. I've tried to convince myself of that too. I've tried to make myself believe that I don't want you, that you are wrong for me, that there was

154

nothing to that night at the farm. But there was, and you know it too." His other hand reached up to grasp the back of her neck and pull her nearer. "I want you so badly it hurts sometimes. And . . ." He lowered his mouth toward hers. "I don't know what to do about it." He kissed her then, a lover's kiss, slow and gentle and persuasive. "Except this," he murmured against her mouth, and she was almost lost once again in the depths of his touch.

But she couldn't be. She had to put a stop to it. She was being tugged further and tighter into his web and she had to find an escape.

She pulled away and stepped back, pressing the back of her hand to her mouth. "I can't, Jake," she whispered. "I just can't."

He watched her closely, while he warred with the impulse simply to overpower her with his strength. "You can, Alison. You want to let go. I know you do. You want to feel something."

Her chin lifted higher in an attempt to combat the truth. "You're wrong," she said, her voice weak with the attempt. "I don't. I have a life of my own back home . . . with my friends. That's the only life I want."

Alison turned and walked away from him, but from behind she heard his voice, clear and low, as he muttered, "Liar." And she knew he was absolutely correct.

CHAPTER ELEVEN

Liar, liar, liar. The word rang in her head over and over and it was what she was hearing now in this new town, at this unfamiliar racetrack, as she watched Jake leaning against the railing studying the race program for the day. He was wearing his racing colors and silks, a dark blue with a white triangle on the left breast, and dark blue bars on white sleeves. A blue-and-white cap sat on the seat of the race cart. His skin looked even more tan against the blue, his eyes dark and warm, his body large and formidable. He really was a handsome man, so full of life, so well liked wherever he happened to be—whether at a racetrack in another town or at home in Bartholomew. As she looked at him now, it wasn't his personality or his kindness or his role as father that caused her to stir inside. What she felt now, what she had felt all along— was only physical. She was convinced of it. It was the dominant factor in her mind; therefore it had to be the only thing there was. Surely he knew that this way of life was not for her. Despite the butterflies that now fluttered out of control inside her stomach and her excitement over Bittersweet's first race; despite the amiable camaraderie in the stable with the other drivers in the race; despite it all, she kept telling herself it was just a stepping-stone to get back into the groove of her real life. This was definitely not the end of the line. This was not where she belonged.

Alison watched Abe crawl up on the gate beside Jake. She started reading the program over his shoulder.

"Looks like there's going to be a lot of early speed in this one," she said.

Alison stepped closer, intrigued by their fascination with the program. "How can you tell?"

"Past performance," Jake answered, still concentrating hard on the list in his hands.

Abe shifted to a more comfortable position. "You'd better lay back at first, Dad."

He nodded slowly, but lifted his eyebrows in speculation. "Unless, of course, everybody else diagnoses it the same way and they all lay back the second the gate leaves."

Alison moved to the other side of Jake and began reading over his left arm. "Do you mean to tell me that all the other drivers are perusing this thing so that they can outguess each other at the starting gate?"

Jake lifted his eyes from the program and grinned at her. "In any game it helps to know your opponent's background and possible moves."

"Doesn't that take all the fun out of it?"

"No, because you can never be too sure what they will do. All you can do is be alert so you can switch tactics if need be."

"Ah," she said, as if she understood what in the heck he was talking about. She didn't.

He turned toward her, his grin slow and intimate. "Spot judgment is most important, you know."

"No," she answered, suddenly weak. "I didn't . . . realize."

"Instinctive reaction . . . and all that," he said, dropping his mouth over hers for a quick kiss that she had no time to counteract. He grinned again. "Just needed that for luck."

Alison caught her breath as he turned back to his program. Why did he always do that to her? Why did her heart begin to pound every time he got close? Why couldn't she remain unaffected by his kisses? She glanced up at Abe, who was watching her closely, a secretive smile touching her mouth. But she, too, turned quickly back to the program and began talking to her father about the race.

"Isn't that guy the troublemaker you were telling me about?" Abe asked, pointing to one of the names on the roster.

"Cowboy Harrigan," Jake whispered back. "He's not really a troublemaker as much as he is stupid. Never knows when his horse is going to break. I'll have to watch out for him. . . . Well," he said, pressing the program into Alison's hands, "guess we'd better do a quick equipment check."

Bittersweet was standing in the aisleway, strapped to the racing sulky. Alison and Abe had been up since early morning, getting her bridled, hobbled, and ready to go.

"How did we do, Dad?" Abe asked, prancing excitedly around the horse.

"Looks pretty good," he murmured, carefully checking that all the lines were buckled and that the hobbles were on correctly. "Boots are buckled properly, nose band is above the nostrils, tail is tied good." He ruffled Abe's hair. "You did good, kiddo."

He stepped past Alison and pinched her chin, winking. "You too, kiddo."

Climbing up onto the sulky, he checked the fit of the handholds.

"How can you be so relaxed?" Alison marveled. He looked as if he were going out for a Sunday ride in his horse-drawn buggy while she, on the other hand, was a bundle of nerves. She had been almost as excited as Abe for the last two days. They had all driven down together in the truck, pulling Bittersweet behind in a trailer, and had stayed in a motel not too far from the county racetrack. She had been the first one up this morning, trying to decide what to wear, wishing that Abe and Jake in the next room would hurry and get up to keep her company. This was the big day. If Bittersweet won, they probably wouldn't have any trouble getting offers to buy her. O happy day! The second half of the inheritance was as good as in her hands.

"No point in getting all stewed up about it," he answered. "She'll either do well or she won't."

"Don't say that." Alison cringed. "That makes me even more nervous."

The smile faded from his face as he looked down at her, studying her closely. "Listen, Alison," he

159

said softly. "I don't want you to put too much hope
. . . I mean, it's the first race I've been in with her
and . . ." He stopped, realizing that nothing he
said was going to lessen the hopes she had for
Bittersweet. He wanted her to win too. At the
same time, he knew that her winning would bring
Alison that much closer to leaving.

"You know she'll win, Jake," Alison said in all
confidence. "Her time has been so good. She can't
lose."

"Well," he said with false brightness. "Guess I'd
better get out there to the paddock."

Abe clambered up onto the sulky and kissed his
cheek. "Good luck, Dad."

"Thanks, kid. See you in the winner's circle." He
clicked the reins and the sulky began to move out
into the sunlight, following the trail of the other
drivers and horses as they headed toward the
track and the beginning post parade.

Abe turned around. "Let's go get a seat, Ali."

It was a hot day in early July, with a dry wind
blowing over the fields. Alison followed Abe up
into the stands, and they found a seat with a good
view. It was stifling in the stands, and the smell of
rusty metal and horse and a thousand people filled
Alison's nose, making it extremely difficult to find
her breath. She closed her eyes to conjure up
sweet smells and cool breezes, but she started
thinking once again about leaving, about what
that would mean to her life. She tried to convince
herself that leaving Abe was the only hard part.
She had grown very accustomed to spending her
days with that precocious and bright little girl, and

she dreaded the inevitable good-byes between them. She refused to believe that leaving Jake would cause her that much pain. They would simply realize that this had been a spring fling, an unusual and brief physical attraction. Yes, that was all it was. Just a passing fancy. Just a touch of spring fever.

Jake led Bittersweet out onto the track, turning her slowly to get her used to the crowd and the noise and excitement. The grandstand was filling up fast, and he glanced up to see if he could spot Alison and Abe. They were putting all their faith in him and expecting him to drive across the finish line first. He didn't want to disappoint them. Especially Alison. He had seen the look in her eyes. She had no doubt that Bittersweet would win. She was convinced of it, and he didn't want to see that happy glow fade away from her. In fact, he had never seen her look so beautiful, and it now tore at his insides.

Bittersweet tried to prance to the side, but he kept her under tight control. She felt the tension, she knew she was expected to perform. He just hoped he wasn't pushing her too fast. But he knew she was ready. Thanks to Abe's surreptitious training sessions, Bittersweet could probably outclass any other horse here today. The real trick was going to be in keeping her in control, keeping her from breaking.

He slipped his stopwatch into his left hand and wrapped the leather thong around his ring finger and then between his index and middle fingers.

The watch now lay comfortably in the palm of his hand so that he could time the eighths and quarters, keeping track of his pace.

He moved on down in line for the post parade, trying to tune out the din of noise coming from the grandstand. This was where the concentration came into play. This was where it was just a driver and a horse.

"It's just you and me now, Bitty, old girl," he murmured, soothing the horse with his steady voice. "Let's give 'em a good show." As soon as the parade of horses was finished, he turned his horse and cart with the other drivers, scoring Bittersweet down easy toward the post gate. "Don't get excited here, girl," he soothed. "It's just the gate. Nothing to get worried about. We'll be out of it in a minute."

The gate was attached to a car and Jake got her right up against the front of it as soon as it began to move. The gate was going pretty slow at the quarter pole, then picked up real speed at the eighth. The starting line was at hand. The gun sounded and the race was under way!

All thoughts of the crowd in the grandstand or of Alison and Abe and their expectations were lost as Jake and Bittersweet barreled into the first turn. The action was all on the track. He looked for a hole at the rail, felt lucky when he found one, and fell into it as quickly as possible. He took some deep breaths, knowing that he might not have time for any more for a while. As they passed the eighth pole, he was fourth in line at the rail. Two horses were parked out and trying to make it to

162

the top. The remaining two in the eight-horse field were trailing at the rail.

Just past the quarter pole, one of the parked horses made it to the top. A driver ahead was beginning to edge away from the rail. But Jake noticed that he was a bit hesitant. He'd have to keep a close eye on him. He could also sense that the driver behind him was thinking about coming around and going ahead of him. It was Cowboy Harrigan. Jake didn't feel comfortable with that guy near him. He didn't like where he was, so he had to make a choice.

In a split second his decision was made. He'd flush out the guy at the rail and try to edge by there. He moved up closer to the one in front and moved a little to the outside, making the driver think he was going to try and pass around. The scheme worked. The driver immediately pulled out to block Jake's path while Jake pulled back in toward the rail. By the three-eighths pole, Jake had flushed him out. As a bonus, he had moved out of the cowboy's dangerous path. Five horses were now at the rail and three on the outside, with two drivers vying for the lead. Jake knew he was in pretty good shape at this point, but he also knew he couldn't let down an inch.

Keeping a tight control on the rein, he eased around the lower turn and headed into the backstretch for the last time. He was going to try to move out around the horse in front of him. With three wide around the final turn, the horse in the lead was tiring and the ones along the rail had nowhere to go.

"Okay, Bitty," he clucked, and she immediately pricked her ears back at the sound of his voice. "This is where we do our stuff. This is what you're made for." He pulled her out and around the two tiring horses on the front end. But Cowboy Harrigan surprised him by pulling from behind. He was now alongside Jake, neck and neck.

In his peripheral vision, he saw Harrigan go to the whip. And Jake was worried. The guy didn't have enough common sense to train a dog, much less a racehorse. Jake had seen him in action too many times before.

They were in the midstretch and he could tell that Bittersweet was tired. But she continued to give a little more than she had, and he kept asking for even more.

From his side, he felt it before he saw it. Harrigan's horse was barreling down alongside, angling in, aiming right for Bittersweet's front leg. Pull her back, you idiot! he silently cried to Harrigan. Pull her back! He felt the sharp clip and gripped the reins tightly as both horses' strides were temporarily broken. It gave two other drivers the edge they needed. One pulled around to the outside to avoid a wreck and ended up taking the lead. Another at the rail got his second wind and pulled up next to the new leader. But Bittersweet didn't let it stop her. Even though she had broken stride and was out of gas, she kept going, pulling up reserves she didn't even know she had. She strode forward, almost staggering. Her head went down and Jake's hands on the reins went with her. He knew that he had to show Bittersweet that he was still with her, that he still had all the confidence in the world in her. His hands on the reins said it all.

Bittersweet came in third across the finish line.

Abe and Alison hurried past the throngs of people, and they were both out of breath by the time they reached their assigned stall.

"She came in third!" Abe cried excitedly, flinging herself at Jake where he was kneeling beside Bittersweet's front leg.

"She only came in third," Alison said, flinging herself dejectedly down onto a steamer trunk.

Jake shot a blank look at her and then lowered his eyes to the horse's leg. "She's hurt," he said.

"What happened to her leg?" Abe asked worriedly, squatting down beside him. Blood was now oozing from a slash that ran two inches up the shin. "How'd she get that?"

Jake poured some antiseptic onto a rag. "Cowboy Harrigan, who else. Hold her for me, will you Abe? This is going to sting." Abe stood up and Alison pulled herself up to come around on the other side to help hold Bittersweet still. Jake pressed the rag against her leg, and the horse tried to move away, but they held her fast. He stood up and wiped a thick band of sweat from his forehead. "I've got to get some X rays," he said. "It doesn't look good."

Another driver came over and knelt down beside Jake. "What's the problem, Koske? Wow, that looks bad," he said when he saw the deep cut. "That happen on the track?"

"Yeah."

Another driver walked up. "Don't tell me, it must have been Harrigan."

Jake looked up at the other driver but didn't answer. It wasn't really necessary. They all knew who caused it, anyway. "I need to get some X rays," he said instead, wanting to focus all his attention on the horse.

"I know a good clinic nearby," one of them said. "It's only about twenty minutes from here. Why don't I give 'em a call and tell 'em that you're on your way?"

"Thanks," Jake said. "I'd appreciate that."

The two men helped him load Bittersweet into the trailer while Abe and Alison stood back in silence and watched. Jake walked over to them before he left.

"You two round up our equipment and have it ready to load onto the truck, okay?"

"Sure, Dad." Abe's eyes were moist, but she was trying very hard not to cry.

Jake saw the look and put his arm around her. "She's going to be all right, Abeline. I'll make sure she's taken care of. I promise." His eyes lifted to Alison. She hadn't said a word and her face was tight and unreadable. "You okay?" he asked gently.

She only nodded. She couldn't even open her mouth to speak. There were just too many questions. So she said nothing as Jake turned and walked over to the truck, checked the trailer door to make sure it was secure, then climbed up into the cab and drove off.

Alison and Abe quietly began gathering up all of the equipment, cleaning it off and storing it in the trunk.

Alison finally broke the silence. "Jake looked worried, didn't he?"

Abe busied herself with the bridle in her hands. "She'll be okay," she answered stiffly. "She just has to be."

Alison watched Abe run her hands over the saddlecloth and collar that Bittersweet had worn in the race, and she understood for the first time just how important that horse was to the girl. For herself, Bittersweet represented only a means to an end. The horse was her way to get what she felt she was due.

But to Abeline Elizabeth Koske, Bittersweet obviously represented something else entirely. Something that Alison could only guess at but never fully understand.

It was three and a half hours later when Jake returned, tired and looking very haggard. Alison pulled a beer can from the cooler and popped the top, handing it over to him. He accepted it in grateful silence. "The muscles have been clipped," he said, the words falling wearily from his mouth.

The sun was on the verge of setting, and to Alison and Abe it felt like he had been gone for days instead of hours. Silence now hung like a shroud among them. No one had the energy or nerve to speak up first.

Alison finally found her voice. "What—what does that mean?"

His eyes slowly lifted to her face, but his expression was held in tight control. "It means she won't race again . . . at least not this year."

"Won't . . . race?" Alison croaked, unable to believe what she was hearing. How could Bittersweet not race? How could Jake sit there so calmly and tell her that the horse who held the strings on her entire life was not going to race?

Abe looped her arms around Jake's waist and pressed her face into his stomach. "I'm sorry, Dad," she whispered, finally letting the tears fall.

His hand stroked soothingly down her hair and along her back. "I'm sorry too, Abeline. I'm so sorry."

Alison stood up, but then lost her wind and sat back down again. "How . . ." The thought trailed away and she had to search for it to pick it up again. "How could this have happened?"

Jake finally lifted his gaze from Abe to Alison. He frowned. "How could what have happened?"

"This—this accident!" Alison realized how unnaturally high her voice sounded, but she had no control over it now. "How could this happen? We have so many more races, so much more to do so that we can sell her. How could she have gotten herself hurt like—" She broke off when she noticed the rock-hard expression that had crept over Jake's face.

"She didn't get herself hurt," he spat. "Another horse ran into her. She showed incredible drive and grit just making it over the finish line the way she did."

"Third place," Alison muttered.

"I don't believe you! You don't give a damn about the horse, do you?" He stepped over to her and grasped her shoulders. "Do you?"

"Jake, let go. You're hurting my arms. Let go!"

"Oh, I'll let go, all right," he growled. "I will definitely let go." He turned around and stalked over to the truck, lowering the tailgate so that he could load the rest of the equipment. He came back for the trunk and stared down pointedly at Alison, waiting for her to stand up so he could get it.

Abe moved up next to him and lightly touched his sleeve. "I don't think Ali meant anything—"

"I know exactly what she meant," he said, fixing Alison with that dark brown stare. "She is thinking of one thing only. Alison McKinsey. Make that two things—Alison McKinsey and money. You don't give a damn about anybody or anything else, do you?"

"That's not true," she insisted. "I'm sorry she's hurt."

"Bull."

Alison lifted her chin and glared back at him. "And—and I suppose you could have been—hurt too."

"You suppose right," he snapped.

"I'm glad you're not."

"Am I supposed to feel honored that you thought about me at all?"

"You're being unfair, Jake."

"Oh," he sneered, "am I?"

"Yes. You're tired and worried and disappointed

and—well, I suppose I'm the likely person to take it out on."

"Don't play the martyr with me, Alison. I know exactly what you're thinking. You're upset because now we won't be able to sell her and—"

"Why not?"

"Why not what?" he snapped.

"Why wouldn't we be able to sell her?"

He looked exasperated. "Who the hell wants to take a risk on a lame horse?"

Her mouth opened and then closed again. When she finally spoke, her voice was whisper-soft. "You mean, no one would want to—to buy her?"

"That's right, Alison," he answered impatiently. "No one."

She glanced at Abe, standing perfectly still as she watched and listened to the bitter exchange. She looked back up at Jake and could barely find her voice. "I have to sell her, Jake."

"Well, good luck," he countered sarcastically. "Let me know when you find the sucker who's willing to pay you for her. Now, could you stand up, so I can load the gear?"

Alison kept clear of him as he hoisted the trunk and carried it out to the truck. She looked over at Abe and could barely keep from cringing. The little girl's eyes were drilling a hole straight through her, boring, penetrating, interrogating. Alison wanted to find the biggest hole she could and crawl into it, hiding from all the questions and needs that one little girl had in her mind.

She glanced toward the truck and saw Jake

standing there, looking back at her. And the realization struck her then. She had lost. Her one chance to take what little she had left and make something of it was gone. She had failed. In the process, she had given away a huge chunk of herself to this man and his little girl. She had lost. But she realized now that she had lost much more than her money. She had lost everything.

She had to go. She had to go back home and forget these people and this life. She had to start over. Her gaze flicked over to Abe, still watching her. She had to go.

And the sooner, the better.

CHAPTER TWELVE

Alison closed her suitcase and set it by the door, then checked around to make sure she hadn't forgotten anything. At the light tap at the door she spun around. "Oh—hi, Abeline. Come on in."

Abe stepped up into the room but hung back by the opening, as if she might want to make a quick exit. "You're all packed up," she said.

"Yes, I think I've got everything."

The girl nodded slowly. "Well, we've got Bitty in the trailer. We're takin' her out to the farm. She'll stay out there until she's better."

"That's good," Alison said, wondering how she could begin to tell this little girl all the things she wanted to tell her. How could she begin to say what she meant to her?

Abe approached the subject first. She was nervously fingering an envelope that was clutched between her hands. "I thought you liked it here, Ali. I thought you liked Bitty."

Alison's breath left her in a painful rush, and it was several moments before she found the courage to speak. "I do, Abeline. It's been fun working with you and . . . and . . ."

"But you're still going to go."

Alison nodded slowly. "Yes. I'm going to go."

"We're gonna fish at the farm this weekend. You might catch one this time . . . if you came."

Alison felt as if her insides were going to split apart and fall to the floor. "Abeline, listen to me. Please. I—I know you don't understand this . . . I don't even understand it very well, but—"

"It's my dad, isn't it? You hate him, don't you?"

"No, Abe, no! I don't hate him at all. We have differences, that's all."

Abe shifted from one foot to the other. "Did—did I do something to make you mad, Ali? I know I bug you about doing my hair and stuff and about all your clothes and—and . . . stuff. But I won't ask you any more dumb questions or anything and . . ."

Alison moved to the girl, dropping down to loop her arms around her and pull her close. It was the first time she had ever hugged Abe, and she wondered now why. Why was it only when she was leaving that she was doing what she had wanted to do all along? She had wanted so many times to hug her, to hold her close and feel her small body against hers. She squeezed tightly now, hoping she could hold back the tears that wanted so badly to fall.

"Abeline," she whispered, still holding her tightly. "I love doing your hair. I've never minded your questions. You are so much fun to be with." She cleared her throat to keep the tears at bay. Holding Abe at arm's length now, she smiled at her. "Abeline, you are very special to me. I like

173

you so much. But I can't stay here. Your father understands this. What is between us is . . . well, it's hard to explain. I want you to understand that it has nothing to do with you. It's me. It is all me. I'm scared, Abe. This place, your father . . . you . . . this isn't the way I thought my life would go. I have no money now. None. And I have to go back to New York to figure out what I'm going to do."

"You could live with us. Dad could take care of you and give you money. You said you wanted somebody to take care of you."

Alison smiled gently. "Yes, I know I said that. But your father doesn't want to support me. He doesn't need me, Abeline. He has you."

"He's a nice man," Abe insisted, trying desperately to make Alison understand. "He really is. I know he drinks a lot and you don't like him living in a stable, but he's really a nice man, Ali. And he's real handsome and everybody likes him and . . ."

Alison held Abe's face between her hands. "I know he's a nice man, Abeline. He's a wonderful man. And yes, he is handsome and—" Her voice broke as she thought of all she was losing by leaving Jake. It was more than physical. She knew that now. It had nothing to do with spring fever. What her body craved from him, her soul craved in triplicate. She loved everything about him. The sound of his voice, the shape of his mouth when he smiled, his easy laughter, his genuine interest in everyone he met. His interest in her.

But he didn't want her here. He had made that plain enough in the last few days. He hadn't even

174

come to tell her good-bye. He would be glad when she was gone.

"Please try to understand, Abe," she said feebly. "I—I have to go."

Abe pulled out of Alison's arms and stood there, scuffling her feet and staring at the floor between them. "I'm supposed to give you this." Her voice was tight as she spoke and then handed the envelope over to Alison.

"What is it?" Alison asked as she tore open the envelope and pulled out a check. She unfolded it and stared in disbelief. It was made out to her in the amount of twenty-five thousand dollars. It was signed *Jake Koske.* "What—I don't understand."

"It's for your half of the horse."

"But—but where did he get it?"

"I dunno. Some bank we went to yesterday."

"Is this the money he's been saving to help buy the farm?"

Abe shrugged and shuffled her feet. "I dunno. I guess."

Alison stared down at the check and then lifted her eyes back to Abe.

"Anyway," the girl mumbled, "guess I better go. Dad's waitin' for me in the truck."

Alison nodded dumbly. "Yes."

She watched as Abe turned without another glance in her direction and walked to the truck. She heard the sound of the truck door as it closed, then the engine starting, and the wheels as they began to turn on the gravel drive, leaving her behind.

She looked down again at the check in her hand.

175

Twenty-five thousand dollars! This would do it. This would show William and the other trustees that at least she could get out what she put into something. It wasn't a profit, but it was her investment in the horse. This would at least show him that she could do that, and that she was not totally frivolous. She had come here a little over a month ago with almost nothing and now she would go back with twenty-five thousand dollars. With this, she could get the rest of her inheritance. She had done it. She had succeeded after all.

She let out a deep sigh and walked over to the cot. She sat down, holding the check loosely in her fingers, and stared at the shiny red floor. The curtain was open and the sunlight streamed in, warming the planks on which it fell. Her head began to shake from side to side. No. She had done nothing. Nothing. Jake had done this. She had had nothing to do with it. He had gone to the bank, had withdrawn twenty-five thousand dollars that he was saving to help purchase his farm. He had given her his money so that she would not go back empty-handed. But she had earned nothing.

Why did he do it? He needed that money. All of his hopes and dreams were tied up in that. His and Abe's plans for the future were wrapped up in that money. So why? Was it because he hoped to be rid of her once and for all? She closed her eyes and let out a slow breath. Oh, God, what had she done? How could she have convinced herself that she needed this money over everything else? This wasn't what she needed at all. Jake was what she needed. His love and his daughter's love were what she really wanted, but she had been afraid to admit it, afraid to believe that she needed anyone's love.

Now it was too late. She was driving to Quincy today to take a plane back home. Jake and Abe had already left for the farm.

No. No, damn it! For once she was going to admit that she was wrong and do something about it. She was not going to make the biggest mistake of her life. She was not going to throw away the best chance she would ever have for love. She was not going to give up Jake Koske.

Throwing her suitcase into the back of the car, she drove out of the fairgrounds, cutting through town and then out onto the highway, hoping her memory would serve her right and show her the way to the farm. She had ridden this way with them several times, but Jake had always been in charge of the driving. She had not had to think about anything. She had done nothing but sit back and let the breeze from the window blow across her face, setting her mind free.

She had spent an hour this morning fixing her hair for the trip home, but now she rolled down the window and let the air billow into the car, and blow through her hair. The fields alternated between dark green and gold, between beans and corn, alfalfa and wheat. The smells were intoxicating, a fragrance that had become so natural to her that she knew she could not be away from it for very long. She needed it. She needed the smells, and the open space, and the freedom, just as she now knew that she needed Jake Koske. She

177

needed him and his little girl. She needed to be a part of their lives.

After what seemed like an eternity, she turned onto the dirt road that led to the property and stopped at the gate. She climbed out of the car, opened the gate, came back and drove through, then climbed out again to close it behind her. She was closing herself in. She knew that. And yet she had never felt less confined or more free in her entire life.

She drove along the road that cut a path through two pastures, crossed the bridge that spanned the thin brown creek, then stopped. The house was straight ahead and she could see Jake and Abe pulling Bittersweet out of the trailer. They led her over to the fence and unhooked the bridle, and Jake gave her an easy pat on the rear. Walking slowly and carefully at first, Bittersweet moved into the pasture of sweet, knee-deep grasses, unsure of herself and of where she was. But within less than a minute, she awkwardly bounded off through the grass, stopped and looked back, and then bolted off again, free and wild among the weeds and wild flowers.

Alison drove straight and deliberately up to the house. The sound of her car door carried to the fence where Jake and Abe were still standing, watching Bittersweet romp over the meadow.

They turned and stared across the yard at her. Neither raised a hand in greeting or made a sound. They simply watched her as she walked over to them and stopped directly in front of Jake.

She held the envelope in her hand. "Why did you do this, Jake?"

He shrugged, holding his expression in check, his voice steady and noncommittal. "It's what you came here for. As you said, this was what you went through"—he swept his hand across the land—"through all of this for. You earned it."

"No, I didn't, Jake. I didn't sell my half of Bittersweet."

"Yes, you did. You just sold it to me."

She hesitated, wondering if perhaps he really didn't want her around. Maybe what she felt was not reciprocated. Maybe she really had been nothing but a spring fling to him. "What if I don't want to sell her to you or to anyone?"

This time he hesitated. "Why wouldn't you want to sell her?"

Alison kept her eyes directly on him, unwavering. "Because I think she would make a fine broodmare. Because I might have to stick around to make sure you do what's best for her." She attempted a smile. "You might decide to take up with Juanita again, and then where would my investment be?"

"You've never worried about your investments before," he said cautiously.

"I'm through standing back and letting other people control my life. I'm taking over for a change."

"You might not be able to do it," he challenged. "You might fall flat on your face."

She saw the hint of a teasing glint come into his

179

eyes, and she smiled. "You'd like that, wouldn't you?"

"Just wondered, that's all."

"Well," she mused, "maybe this time I could find a good man to stand behind me, sort of prop me up."

"There aren't too many good men around here," he pointed out.

"Oh, I don't know. I know of one fairly decent fellow."

He still hadn't cracked a smile. "Anyone I know?"

"Probably not." She shrugged and looked off toward the field. "This guy's been hiding out in a tack room, if you can imagine that." She glanced down at Abe and winked. "He and some bratty kid. A real ornery duo." She lifted her eyes back to Jake and her face grew serious. "They have this really bad habit of making poor, helpless women fall in love with them. They're really—"

Before she could finish, Jake closed the slim space between them and pulled her into his arms, holding her fiercely against him as if he would never let go. "God, but do you have any idea what you've put me through! Do you have any earthly idea?"

She was crushed against him and the low growl of his voice vibrated against her chest. "It's taken me a long time to come to my senses, Jake. I've been an idiot. I've been living my whole life on the run. I'm so tired of it. You're the only person who's ever shown me anything different. A better way."

He held her at arm's length and shook his head.

"I've wanted so many times to ask you to stay. To beg you or force you, but I knew what you'd say. I didn't think you wanted to be here." He let out a long sigh. "I know you've been pulled all your life. I just didn't want to be guilty of doing the same thing to you."

"What would you have done if I'd gone back to New York? Would you have just let me go?"

He sighed again. "Probably. I'm a stubborn man, Alison."

"I didn't know that."

He glanced up to see her grinning at him. He sighed again, this time in relief. His gaze shifted to the meadow. "Bitty seems to like it out here."

"Yes," Alison said, switching her gaze to the horse. "She does, doesn't she. Well, some of us need that free and wild life." She looked back at Jake, but he wasn't smiling. He was studying her carefully.

"For how long, Alison? How long will you need it? And will you get tired of it?"

"I don't think there are any pat answers, Jake."

He nodded slowly. "You're right. I guess that was unfair of me."

"No, it wasn't unfair. You have every right to question that. It's just that I'm not sure how to answer it. It is what I want right now, and therefore I assume it's what I'll always want. But how can we be sure?"

He laid his hand against her cheek. "We can't, Alison. We can't be sure of anything. If nothing else, I should have learned that much in life. I'm just grateful we have a chance to be together now. I hope it will be forever."

"So do I. But, you know, I do have to go back to New York to get everything straightened out with my attorney."

"I know."

"Will you go with me?"

Jake shook his head. "No, Alison. That's something you have to do on your own."

"Why?"

"Because I want your decision to come back to be your own. If I'm there with you, the choice would not be all yours."

"I will come back, you know."

He nodded. "I believe you." He glanced down at the envelope in her hand. "What are you going to do with that?"

"It's yours, Jake."

"But I want you to have it."

"Why?" He shifted his eyes toward the pasture where Bittersweet had stopped to graze, and Alison saw the flinch in his jaw. "Are you unsure of why I want to stay with you?"

He kept his eyes toward the field. "I don't know, Alison. This money has always been so important to you. I don't know what you want anymore."

"I've always wanted money for the wrong reasons, Jake. For money's sake alone, for power, for the accumulation of material things. And yet I was never happy. Never until I came here and learned to live on nothing. For heaven's sake, I've been living in a stable and I've never been happier."

"And what about now? What about all that

money you thought should be yours, that you wanted so badly?"

"Now?" She shrugged. "The only reason I would want it now is for the freedom it could give us. You and me and Abe. With it, we could buy this farm, Jake. We could buy some horses and start a breeding business."

"We could start the way other people do," he said. "From the bottom. I'm a veterinarian. I'm good. I made good money when I worked at it, and I will again."

"I know you will," she said. "But this could help. It could bring the dream a little closer."

"I'm not saying it wouldn't be nice to have that money," he said. "To put it to use that way. But I don't want it to come between us."

"And you think it might?"

He nodded slowly. "Yes, I think it might."

She studied him thoughtfully. "What if we were to take just enough to make a down payment on the property, just to get a start? And the rest we could put into a trust . . . for Abeline . . . and for any—well—other children that might—well—come along."

He was staring at her and a slow smile began to edge across his face. "You would do that . . . for my daughter?"

"Of course. She would be my daughter too." She cocked her head and rested her hands on her waist. "I hope you don't think I was planning to live out here with you 'in sin,' as they say. I can just imagine how that would go over in Bartholomew."

Jake was staring at her, smiling in wonderment. "Do you have any idea how much I love you?"

She smiled. "Yes, I think so."

"I've got to teach you everything, you know. You've got to learn to fish and raise horses and help me deliver foals." He reached up and touched her face again. "I've got to teach you everything."

"Aren't you supposed to kiss or something?" the small voice beside them asked. They both looked over at Abe, standing with her hands shoved into the pockets of her overalls. They had been so wrapped up in each other that they had forgotten she was standing there, listening to it all.

Jake chuckled. "You know, kid, you're absolutely right." He reached for Alison and pulled her next to him. "But first," he said, looking sideways down at Abe, "what would you think about Alison and me getting married? You think that would be all right?"

Abe slipped her hands into the suspenders of her overalls and rocked back on her heels, her eyes narrowed in speculation on the two grown-ups waiting for her answer. "Well, that depends," she began, and both Jake's and Alison's eyes were riveted on that small, pensive face. "When we fix up the house, do I get to paint my room red?"

Jake's mouth dropped open and he turned to stare at Alison, still holding her against him. "Do you mean to tell me . . ." He paused and shook his head, as if clearing it from some overpowering fog. "Am I going to have to live in a red house!"

Alison tilted her head back and laughed, then pressed her lips against Jake's, warming his mouth with her own. When she finally released him, she grinned. "You don't expect me to live in this gray gloom without a little color, do you?"

He turned toward the house and lifted his hands and arms in a shrug. "Good-bye white house. Good-bye simple country charm. Good-bye peace and quiet." He paused dramatically and let his arms drop to his sides. "Alison McKinsey is movin' in."

He turned to her smiling face, wrapped one arm around her shoulder and the other around Abe's. Together the three of them started walking toward the house. Abe grinned up at them. "Well, all I can say is it's about time you two started acting like grown-ups. I'm sick and tired of being the only one around here who knows what's going on all the time. Oh, look at that!" she cried, dashing off in a flurry to chase a couple of ground squirrels.

Alison turned to Jake and wrapped her arms around his waist. "Amazing, isn't it, that she saw what we couldn't see. Guess we can learn a lot from a ten-year-old kid."

Jake ran his hands up and down her back. "Not everything, though. We've got a few things to learn from each other first."

She grinned mischievously. "Oh, I don't know. I'm not so sure you know anything that I don't know. I've seen all of your moves."

His chuckle was deep and husky. "You don't know us wild country boys very well. We've got moves you eastern city slickers never even heard of."

She snuggled closer. "Sounds wonderful. So how

long is it going to take you to teach me all of them?"

"Oh, fifty years at least."

"Is that all, Jake Koske? Only fifty years? Ha, and I thought you said you had lots of moves." She pulled out of his arms, looked bored as she checked her fingernails. "Can't be that many if it only takes fifty years."

In one fell swoop, he had her in his arms, carrying her through the open doorway into the parlor. He kicked the door shut with his boot. "It's just a damn good thing I've got a well-mannered kid who knows to knock before entering." He set Alison on her feet and pulled her to him, bending his head to press his lips against her throat. "Now," he groaned, "if I can just teach my future wife some manners."

Her head fell back and her breath grew ragged and quick. "Manners are not what I had in mind," she whispered, looping her hands around his neck.

"No," he moaned urgently. "Me either."

"So . . ." Her pulse began to pound and she searched for her breath. "This is . . . lesson one?"

His mouth moved over hers in a rough caress. "Yeah, take notes now."

"I have a wonderful memory." She sighed as his hand lifted to cover her breast.

"And we'll have lots of practice," he murmured, smiling against her lips. "Fifty years at least."

She grabbed a handful of his hair and held him close, smiling back. "Oh, no, you don't. You're not getting away from me that soon. Now that I've got

186

you, I'm not letting go. This house will fall before we will."

His fingers eased open the buttons of her blouse. "So you think you can live here in this place . . . I mean, every day?"

"And night, Koske," she whispered. "Let's talk about the nights."

Outside, the afternoon sun burned brightly, spreading its light over the fields and meadows. Abe stood up on the fence and clutched Bittersweet's neck in utter abandonment and joy, complete and whole in her world once again, while inside . . .

"Oh, yes," Jake murmured huskily, lowering Alison slowly to the floor with him. "Let's talk about the nights." His mouth moved urgently over her parted lips. "Let's definitely talk about the nights."

A beautiful book
for the special people
who still believe in
love . . .

RICHARD BACH'S

The Bridge Across Forever

By the same
author who
created
_Jonathan
Livingston
Seagull,
Illusions,_
and _A Gift
of Wings._

10826-8-44 $3.95

Rebels and outcasts, they fled halfway across the earth to settle the harsh Australian wastelands. Decades later—ennobled by love and strengthened by tragedy—they had transformed a wilderness into fertile land. And themselves into

The Australians

WILLIAM STUART LONG

THE EXILES, #1	12374-7-12	$3.95
THE SETTLERS, #2	17929-7-45	$3.95
THE TRAITORS, #3	18131-3-21	$3.95
THE EXPLORERS, #4	12391-7-29	$3.95
THE ADVENTURERS, #5	10330-4-40	$3.95
THE COLONISTS, #6	11342-3-21	$3.95

Now you can reserve April's
Candlelights
<u>before</u> they're published!

- ♥ You'll have copies set aside for *you* the instant they come off press.
- ♥ You'll save yourself precious shopping time by arranging for *home delivery*.
- ♥ You'll feel proud and efficient about organizing a system that *guarantees* delivery.
- ♥ You'll avoid the disappointment of not finding *every* title you want and need.

ECSTASY SUPREMES $2.75 each

- ☐ 117 **DESERT PRINCESS**, H. Monteith 11895-6-22
- ☐ 118 **TREASURE FOR A LIFETIME**, L. Vail 18758-3-15
- ☐ 119 **A DIFFERENT KIND OF MAN**, B. Andrews . . 12039-X-19
- ☐ 120 **HIRED HUSBAND**, M. Catley 13646-6-12

ECSTASY ROMANCES $2.25 each

- ☐ 418 **GYPSY RENEGADE**, M. Lane 13280-0-13
- ☐ 419 **A HINT OF SPLENDOR**, K. Clark 13610-5-14
- ☐ 420 **DOCTOR'S ORDERS**, P. Hamilton 12074-8-15
- ☐ 421 **RACE THE WIND**, V. Flynn 17232-2-39
- ☐ 422 **FORTUNE HUNTER**, C. Kenyon 12665-7-28
- ☐ 423 **A WOMAN'S TOUCH**, K. Whittenburg 10513-7-26
- ☐ 424 **MIDNIGHT SECRETS**, K. Daley 15619-X-10
- ☐ 425 **TONIGHT YOU'RE MINE**, E. Delatush 18988-8-17

At your local bookstore or use this handy coupon for ordering:

**DELL READERS SERVICE—DEPT. B994D
P.O. BOX 1000, PINE BROOK, N.J. 07058**

Please send me the above title(s). I am enclosing $_____ (please add 75c per copy to cover postage and handling). Send check or money order no cash or CODs Please allow 3-4 weeks for shipment. CANADIAN ORDERS please submit in U.S. dollars

Ms Mrs Mr _____

Address_____

City State_____ Zip _____